THE MISTLETOE HOUSE

A CHESTNUT COVE CHRISTMAS NOVEL

MIA KENT

The Mistletoe House

By Mia Kent

WANT TO BE A VIP READER?

Join my Reader Club for all the latest news on upcoming releases, special savings, fun announcements, sneak peeks, and more—delivered right to your inbox! Visit www.miakent.com/readerclub to sign up.

CHAPTER 1

"It's not that I don't love you, Natalie. I do. I just don't think you're... you know. The one."

Mug of coffee clutched in one hand, edge of the table clutched in the other, Natalie Belmont stared at Devin in disbelief over her scrambled eggs. "I'm not the one? I'm not the *one*? What does that even mean, Devin? And what about the past seven years?"

He shifted uncomfortably in the chair across from her, his eyes on his plate instead of on her face as he toyed with a piece of bacon. The piece of bacon that *she'd* cooked for him, thank you very much. "Like I said," he murmured to the tablecloth, "it's not that things haven't been, um, good. They have. But I want to get married, I want to start a family, and—"

"But I want all those things too." Natalie's fork fell from her fingers with a clatter, but she barely registered it. Her hand felt numb. Her whole body felt numb, because this couldn't be happening. Her fiancé, the man she had loved for most of her thirties, the man she lived with and worked with and built a *life* with… he couldn't possibly be breaking up with her at eight-thirty on a Sunday morning over the breakfast she'd gotten up early to prepare for him, just the way he liked it. Not because she felt obligated, but because she loved him. Because he *was* "the one."

"I know you do." Devin was now speaking to the butter dish. "But I've decided that I no longer want those things with, um… you."

That last word was a gong resounding throughout the room, and Natalie's temples throbbed as she tried to make sense of the impossible. She and Devin had been together—and happy—for more than half a decade now, since not long after she began working as the manager in the ice cream shop he owned and operated in the city. It was love at first sight for her, and even though she knew better than to fall for a coworker, let alone her boss, their first kiss had been inevitable. Since then, they hadn't spent a single day apart, and this past summer, he'd dropped to one knee in front of a carousel at their favorite park and asked him to be hers forever.

And now, less than six months later...

How? Why?

Natalie dreaded the next question, the one that needed to be vocalized, and a tremor of fear shot through her as she asked, "Is there someone else?"

Someone better, she wanted to say, but didn't. Someone less damaged.

For so long, Devin had been the very best part of her. He'd picked up the broken, jagged pieces of her past and helped her glue them back together, one by one, until she could finally call herself happy. Until she could finally call herself free.

The walls felt like they were closing in on her as she held her breath, waiting for his response, and only then did Devin raise his gaze to meet hers, his blue eyes unbearably sad. "There isn't anyone else," he said softly. "I would never do that to you. But for me, things just haven't felt... right... in a long time. I'm almost forty, and so are you. We need to be thinking about our future, the things we want. And as much as I've enjoyed our time together, I just don't see us growing old together."

Well. Pretty hard to come back from *that* one.

The tears were sliding down Natalie's cheeks as she pushed herself back from the table, her chair legs making an unholy screech against the linoleum, the rest of the scrambled eggs wobbling in the pan she'd set between them. "So sorry I've wasted your time. And I'm even sorrier that you've wasted mine."

Head bowed, heart ripped in half, she made a beeline for their bedroom, throwing herself to the floor and yanking her suitcase out from beneath the bed. She slammed it down on the comforter and unzipped it roughly, then began tearing clothes from her wardrobe and shoving them inside, eyes clouded with tears, unaware of what she was even packing. The bathroom came next, with Natalie clearing the sink with a sweep of her arms, jars of makeup and bottles of lotion tumbling from her hands as she hurled them into the suitcase. Finally, she pulled open the top drawer of her nightstand and carefully removed the red velvet box, her most precious, most prized possession, and gently tucked it into the suitcase between two shirts, checking and double-checking that it was safe.

Then, with a glance out the window, and a groan at the sight of snowflakes gently falling from the gray-blue sky, she grabbed her peacoat from where it was flung across the back of a chair and stuffed her arms in the sleeves unceremoniously.

"You don't have to do this, you know." Natalie jumped, and turned to find Devin leaning against the doorframe, his face grave as he watched her pack. "I'm headed to my folks' house for a few weeks to celebrate the holidays—Kent is going to make sure things are running smoothly at the shop."

At the sound of her coworker's name, the rest of the breath rushed out from Natalie's lungs all at once. Her relationship, gone. Her home, gone—the townhouse belonged to Devin; she'd given up the lease on her apartment long ago. And now, her job, the thing she loved most in her life besides Devin... presumably, gone. Devin spent most of his time at the ice cream shop; the last thing he would want was to share the space with his ex.

Natalie swallowed hard to dissolve the rapidly spreading lump in her throat, then, with great difficulty, forced herself to meet his eyes. "Is Kent... will he be running things now?"

Devin nodded. "I thought it was for the best," he said quietly. "That way, you can move on." A pause, then, "Both of us can."

The basketball in her throat was back, and Natalie was taking deep, steadying breaths in a vain attempt to calm herself. Of course this would happen only a few weeks before Christmas. Of *course* it would, because nothing good happened this time of year. This was why Natalie avoided celebrating the holiday at all costs. For her, it was draped in grief and loss, sadness and an uncertain future. Thirty years had passed, and nothing had changed.

"Anyway." Devin cleared his throat. "Like I said, I'm going to be with my parents for a while, so the place is yours until I come back. That should give you enough time to make other... arrangements." He winced, and Natalie made a strangled sound somewhere between a laugh and a sob.

"You think a few weeks is enough time for me to find a new place to live, a new job, and... what, Devin? An entirely new life? How generous of you. How thoughtful."

Her voice was rising to a fever-pitch, and she was seconds away from picking up the framed photo of them beside the bed and hurling it at his face. "You're a great guy, Devin, you know that?" she spat at him. "A stand-up man. You should win an Olympic medal. Gold, for world's biggest a—"

"Natalie, come on. Don't be like this." Devin folded his arms and frowned at her, as if *she* were the one being unreasonable here. "Let's just respect each other, okay? Get through this amicably."

Natalie did laugh then, though it had a maniacal edge to it, and without further ado, she hoisted the suitcase off the bed, jammed it on the floor, and rolled it past him, not bothering to ask him to move. "Oof," he said, wincing and rubbing his leg where she'd accidentally-on-purpose rammed it against him. He sidestepped her quickly, then followed her as she stomped down the hallway, the tears still falling thick and fast—as fast as the snowflakes swirling through the morning sky.

"Great," she muttered to herself as she wrenched open the front door, her lungs shocked by the sudden burst of frigid air. "Bad weather. Just what I need right now."

Indeed, a gossamer-thin layer of snow had already accumulated on the street and the windshield of her car, and she brushed away the latter with the sleeve of her coat before hoisting her suitcase into the trunk and sliding in behind the wheel. Devin was still standing in the doorway, looking as forlorn as an abandoned puppy, and Natalie's breath was puffing out in clouds around her as she debated whether one middle finger or two would do the trick.

No, she thought fiercely. No, she wouldn't give him the satisfaction. She wouldn't give him the—

Then he raised his hand in a goodbye wave before blowing her a kiss, the way he always did before she left to go somewhere, and she decided that two would most *definitely* do. Or three, if she could have contorted her feet that way.

She didn't look up to see his reaction; instead, she focused on breathing, and sliding the keys into the ignition, and trying to figure out where in the world she was going. She couldn't run home, like Devin, because she had no home. Not really, although the Sandersons told her when she left that she'd always be welcome with them, part of their perfect, shining family. They had been lovely people, really, and based on the horror stories she'd heard some foster kids swapping, she knew she was lucky to have been placed with them after her grandmother's death.

But the Sandersons had their kids, and Natalie wasn't one of them.

The snow was falling thicker now, more urgent, and other drivers were beginning to turn on their headlights despite the early hour. Natalie flicked on the windshield wipers, momentarily soothed by the rhythmic back-and-forth motion as she debated her options... of which, admittedly, there were few.

Random hotel? Maybe. Flight to Hawaii? In her dreams. All Natalie knew was that she needed to get out of the city, far from the home she and Devin shared, away from the scene of so many of her most blissful memories. She had no one to stay with. All of her friends were here, and besides, they were Devin's friends too, and each and every one of them was part of a couple, smug in their togetherness.

Natalie couldn't bear it.

She sighed. The Sandersons it was, then. At least Jennifer and Todd had been understanding of the whole Christmas... thing. They never forced holiday activities on her, never tried convincing her to build gingerbread houses or ice cookies shaped like candy canes. Each Christmas Eve, they'd given her a few small gifts, and didn't complain when she spent the rest of the night and much of the following day in her room, trying her best to distract herself.

Pulling out her cell phone, Natalie swiped to her contacts list and typed out a quick message to Jennifer, who responded immediately, and enthusi-astically. *Our door is always open to you, sweetheart. You know that.* She stared down at the words for a while, her eyes brimming with tears, then keyed the

Sandersons' address into the GPS and waited for it to calculate.

Six hours.

Six hours driving through snow, with a broken heart.

Merry Christmas, Natalie thought, pulling into traffic, refusing to glance back at the place that, just thirty minutes ago, she had called home. *And a crappy New Year.*

CHAPTER 2

wo hours later, Natalie was stuck in bumper-to-bumper traffic on a snow-covered highway in the middle of nowhere, flicking through the radio, trying to find a station—*any* station would do—that wasn't playing Christmas music. The mountains on either side of the highway were draped in a thick, unyielding white, and the windshield wipers on her car were whipping back and forth manically, trying and failing to keep up with the relentless snowfall.

What was going on here? Not for the first time, Natalie craned her neck past the eighteen-wheeler in front of her to see why traffic had been locked in a near-standstill for the past forty-five minutes. The drivers in the cars on either side of her were begin-

MIA KENT

ning to look irate, and she couldn't blame them—not only was the heater in her car barely functioning at this point, but the heavy snow pounding down from the sky was no match for the salted roads and had begun piling up at an alarming rate. If this kept up much longer, they would all be trapped.

But something worse was happening, too. Something much, much worse.

Natalie averted her eyes to avoid looking at the little red "check engine" light that had been flickering on and off on her dashboard for the past two hours... okay, fine, for the past three weeks, and why, oh *why*, had she spent so much time ignoring it? There was always somewhere more important to go, something more urgent to do, and besides, Devin had a car and they worked at the same place, so if hers conked out for a few days, no harm, no foul. Right?

Wrong. So wrong, and she had no one to blame but herself.

Please, she silently begged whoever might be listening. *Please don't make this day any worse.* At this rate, she wouldn't make it to the Sandersons' house until well after nightfall, and the adrenaline of the past few hours already had exhaustion setting in.

The traffic inched forward, the snow fell faster

and harder, and that little red light continued to taunt her. Thoughts of Devin threatened to fill her head, but Natalie did her best to squash them down, knowing that right now wasn't the time to try and unpack what had gone wrong with their relationship. Besides, there was every chance he would change his mind, because she knew that he hadn't been pretending to love her for the past seven years —no one was that good of an actor. Maybe he just needed time, she decided. Time, and a little bit of perspective.

Then he would undoubtedly come crawling back, and after a proper amount of cold-shouldering, she would let him.

"New route found," a robotic voice blared in the car, causing Natalie to nearly jump out of her skin. *"Avoids three-hour slowdown."* She glanced down at her GPS screen to find it offering to recalculate her route, and she immediately punched the *accept* button. *"Take exit 48 in two-tenths of a mile,"* the voice squawked.

Squinting through the thick flakes still pouring down like raindrops, Natalie could barely make out the exit sign a little way ahead. Judging by the pace she was moving, she'd be there in, oh, say, another hour? Then she eyed the shoulder of the highway, and after a quick glance in all directions to check for a police car, she jerked her steering wheel to the right, nearly hitting the back of the eighteen-wheeler as she squeezed past it and found herself blissfully free.

She made it to the exit in a flash, ignoring the death stares of her fellow drivers, and saw that the relatively snow-free road that stretched ahead of her wound up the side of the mountain and was bordered on either side by enormous pine trees whose boughs seemed to brush the heavens. It was a magnificent sight—much better than the bumper of that eighteen-wheeler—and better yet, the road was completely deserted.

Up, up, up she went, gazing at the scenery in awe as she drove past an overlook and saw the thick groves of trees that covered the mountain in all directions, their leaves glittering with new-fallen snow. The sky overhead was a crisp, clear blue, and every now and then, she saw a deer darting through the woods beside the road, nothing more than a flash of brown amidst the white. Besides her, there wasn't a soul in sight, and any twinges of concern she may have felt were immediately dispelled by Natalie's regular checks of the GPS screen, which continued to assure her that she was on the right course.

A good thing, too, because the "check engine" light was now a steady red warning, and her car had begun making a low, insistent whining sound that she could almost—*almost*—pretend she couldn't hear over the muffled country song playing from the staticky radio. But that was fine, of course, perfectly fine, because in just a few miles, she'd be off this deserted road, and surely she'd make it to the Sandersons' house with her car fully intact, because it had been her faithful companion for a decade now, and it would not—she repeated, would *not*—let her down. Not now. Not here.

A bump jolted her back to attention, and Natalie realized that she had left the paved road and was now on what looked like a narrow dirt path, barely big enough for a car, nearly hidden by the thick layer of snow that was accumulating despite the dense evergreen branches that crisscrossed overhead.

"This can't be right," she muttered to herself, squinting down at the GPS, which stared back at her placidly, reassuringly. The route showed that she was near the top of the mountain, and in a few more miles, she would descend to a different highway, apparently bypassing the slowdown altogether. With a glance at the warning light, and a nervous pat to the dashboard along with a few whispered words of encouragement, she navigated the first part of the dirt road while clutching the wheel for dear life. The car bumped over rocks and fallen branches, and at one point bottomed out with an alarming scraping sound that had her squeezing her eyes shut in fear.

But she and the car continued trundling along just the same, and as a patch of sunlight emerged from the thick cover of trees, and the road began its long, snaking descent down the mountain, she released the tense breath she'd been holding. "You did good, girl," she said, giving the dashboard another fond pat. "I'll get you to the mechanic as soon as I can, and you'll have a nice checkup."

The car must have registered those last words as permission to finally rest, because after one last long, loud whine, the engine spluttered once and then died altogether.

"Oh no," Natalie said into the sudden silence. "Oh no, oh no, oh *no*." She pounded her fist against the dashboard, then the steering wheel, then the passenger seat, just for good measure. Then she removed the keys from the ignition and jammed them in again, hoping for a different outcome.

Silence, except for the jackhammering of her heart.

She was screwed. She was so, *so* screwed, because she was completely and utterly alone, and... yep. Her cell phone wasn't getting any reception either, because this was the single worst day in the history of the world.

Natalie kicked open the driver's door and immediately began shivering in her peacoat as she pried open the hood of the car and stared blankly at the many internal... thingies. She didn't know how to change a tire, let alone diagnose and fix a dire problem, and did she mention she was screwed?

It didn't take long for panic to start setting in, her breathing ragged and uneven as she debated her options. As she saw it, there were two of them:

Stay where she was and freeze to death.

Walk as far as she could down the mountain and freeze to death.

Tears were useless, because they were already hardening on her lashes, making her—if possible—even colder. Grabbing her purse from the passenger seat, along with the spare blanket she kept in the back, Natalie began walking back the way she had come, her tennis shoes slipping and sliding on the icy path. The world around her was entirely, eerily silent, not even a bird trilling in the trees overhead or a squirrel scampering through the undergrowth.

Before long, her feet were simultaneously numb and on fire, and a deep, throbbing ache had started in her bare hands, which were shoved in the pockets of her peacoat. Even though it felt like she had been walking for miles—for eons, maybe—when she turned back, her car was still in sight, a bright red smear against the backdrop of pure white.

Shivering from head to toe, she continued trudging forward, every so often tripping over a tree root embedded in the path, her mind wandering to dark, shadowy places as she tried not to think about what would happen if no one were to find her.

Which wouldn't happen... right? Because surely *someone* had driven this road before. Surely she wasn't the only idiot out there. In fact, Natalie was so certain that she'd hear the rumble of an engine at any moment that she continuously strained to hear it through the thick silence that blanketed the even thicker forest. But the only sound she heard was the occasional puff of her own breathing as she navigated the lonely road, the drumbeat of fear growing louder by the second.

Thirty minutes passed, and then an hour, and by now, Natalie's feet were burning so intensely from the cold that her walk was reduced to a hobble. Deciding to reserve at least some of her strength, she found an overturned tree, draped her blanket over the trunk to provide some measure of protection from the snow, and then hoisted herself onto it. She gazed over the stunning yet forlorn landscape, then checked and rechecked her phone several more times before shoving it back inside her purse with a sigh. Still no signal.

She would rest for a few minutes, she decided, and then continue down the mountain until she had reception—she would slide down the mountain on her bottom if she had to, because this was *not* how it ended. This was not what was written on her tombstone, no sir, because she had things to do. Get married, for one—though that now seemed depressingly out of reach. Have children… which, yep, even further.

Be happy?

Yes, that would do. What Natalie wanted, above all else, was to be happy, though that feeling had eluded her for most of her life. She thought she'd finally found that with Devin. In fact, she'd been sure of it.

But as Natalie well knew, it only took an instant for everything to change.

The sun was high in the sky now, and Natalie turned her face up to it, reveling in whatever scant warmth it could provide. A bird was singing somewhere in the branches above her, which she took as a good sign, and so it was with a renewed burst of energy that she hopped down from the tree trunk, rolled her soggy blanket into a ball that she stuffed under one arm, and began trudging through the snow once more.

Shimmering flakes were still whirling and twirling through the air around her, though the snow was less urgent now, more light and peaceful. Instinctively, she caught one in her bare hand, taking a moment to admire its intricate beauty, and had just caught a second, then a third, when a distinct roar cut through the impossible quiet around her.

The unmistakable sound of an engine, growing louder and more insistent.

It was all Natalie could do not to drop to the snow on her knees and weep.

She was saved. Not by a Christmas miracle, because she knew those didn't exist. But by some kind of miracle all the same.

CHAPTER 3

The pickup truck rumbled to a stop beside her, the man inside cutting the engine and hopping out, his dark eyes both curious and concerned as they swept Natalie up and down. "Hey there," he said, glancing around, his mouth turned down in a slight frown. "Are you out here alone?"

Natalie hesitated. Now that she wasn't alone, she was keenly aware that she actually *was* alone—alone, in the middle of nowhere, with a complete stranger and no one else around to hear her screams. She eyed him nervously. He didn't *look* like a murderer, but wasn't that what a murderer would want her to think? His jeans were muddy from the knees down, he wore heavy-duty hiking boots, and a thermal shirt peeked out from beneath his thick winter coat. His brown hair was mostly hidden beneath a ski hat, but his beard was trimmed and his eyes were kind.

Option three, Natalie decided: don't freeze to death, but end up stuffed in the back of a stranger's pickup alongside the freshly cut pine tree he seemed to be bringing home.

The man's eyebrows were now furrowed in confusion, and Natalie realized she hadn't spoken a single word, not even a hello.

"Um."

She cleared her throat, eyeing the single deserted road that wound back down the mountain. The highway was nowhere near visible from here, which meant she had several hours of walking ahead of her... if she made it that far without succumbing to the frigid temperatures.

Sensing her unease, the man smiled, his eyes crinkling pleasantly at the corners. He looked to be about her age, somewhere in his late thirties, and... okay, so he was pretty cute. Somewhere between a lumberjack and an Eskimo, and either Natalie was beginning to find that incredibly appealing, or she was becoming delirious. As if on cue, she shivered violently, and the man's smile fell from his face.

"You look miserable. Here, come inside the truck

and warm up. I've been out for a couple hours finding the perfect Christmas tree, so I'm halfway to a snowman myself. I've got the heater on full blast, and there's even a thermos of hot chocolate in there if you're thirsty."

As he was speaking, the man rounded the pickup truck and pulled open the passenger door, showering the road with even more snow. He gave her an expectant look. "I won't hurt you. I promise." Then he held up a finger. "Hang on, I have an idea." Reaching inside the truck, he yanked the keys from the engine, then tossed them to her. "It won't be as warm in there without the heater running, but you'll have complete control. I have a sister, so believe me, I get it. My father started drilling safety tips into her head when we were kids."

He grinned at her, and Natalie could feel some of her unease slipping away. "Thanks," she said, gazing down at the keys, turning them over in her hand. She jerked her thumb down the road. "I broke down somewhere back there. I was on the highway, and my GPS decided this route would be a good time-saver. Apparently, my car didn't agree."

"Ah, another GPS casualty." He gave a knowing nod. "You're hardly the first. Vernon's been kept pretty busy this season with wayward travelers

23

looking for a shortcut." Shaking his head, he sighed. "Problem is, if you don't know these mountains, you can run into a whole heap of trouble."

Natalie snorted. "I found that out the hard way, but I feel like less of a moron knowing I'm not alone." She cocked her head at him. "Who's Vernon?"

"He's our mechanic. He's also our tow truck driver." The man reached inside the truck and produced a thermos, then approached Natalie and handed it to her. "Go on, have a drink. It was my mother's recipe, and it's the best." He watched while she took a sip, her breath escaping on a sigh of satisfaction as the hot chocolate hit her lips. He was right; it was delicious, the best she'd ever had, rich and creamy with the perfect balance of marshmallows and even a hint of mint.

"Thank you," she said, handing the thermos back to him. "I was starting to turn into a human popsicle out here. It's a good thing you came along, or I don't know what would have happened." She gestured to her relatively thin winter coat and tennis shoes. "I'm not exactly dressed for mountain climbing."

"No." He chuckled. "I'd say not." Then he nodded toward the truck. "If you want to hop in, I'll bring you into town, and we can figure out what to do about your car."

She glanced at the truck, then at him, still not entirely convinced. "Maybe I'd better wait here for Vernon to come. That way he can..." But she trailed off when she saw the man shaking his head.

"He probably won't make it out until tomorrow morning, earliest." He glanced at his watch. "At this time on a Sunday afternoon, he's almost definitely taking a nap." Seeing her surprise, he added, "Chestnut Cove is a small town, so time runs a little differently here. Most of us still respect the idea of Sunday as a rest day, which I know is probably a pretty foreign concept to the rest of the country."

"No, I think it's great," Natalie said, and meant it. Then she laughed. "I mean, I'd think it was great if my car didn't decide to break down on a Sunday." Chewing her bottom lip, she considered the truck. It did look awfully warm in there, and so far, nothing about this man screamed creepy. Or murderous.

"Okay," she said, finally relenting, because what other choice did she have? "I'd love a ride to town, if you don't mind taking me."

"It's no trouble at all." He nodded toward the keys still tucked in Natalie's hand. "You want to drive? That way you'd feel more comfortable."

"No." She laughed. "Believe me, all three of us would end up going off the side of the mountain—

25

you, me, and your truck. It was a harrowing drive up here, to say the least."

"These roads do take practice," he acknowledged. "As soon as I turned sixteen, my father had me out here in every kind of condition so I learned how to navigate them." He slid off one of his gloves and held out a hand—a very nice hand, Natalie decided, taking it. "I'm Gabe, by the way. Gabe Archer. It's nice to meet you…?"

"Natalie," she supplied. "Natalie Belmont. And… thank you. I really appreciate the help."

She rounded the truck to the passenger side, and was just about to open the door when Gabe slid a hand around her and did it for her. He waited until she'd climbed in, then handed her the seatbelt and shut her firmly inside. As he headed to the driver's side, Natalie reached across the dashboard to slot the keys into the ignition, and glorious heat immediately began blasting through the truck's interior.

"How far is town?" she asked when he'd climbed inside and settled himself behind the wheel. "I've never heard of Chestnut Cove. In fact," she added, looking around at the snow-tipped pine trees that covered the mountain as far as the eye could see, "I have no idea where I am right now. I'm directionally-challenged on a good day, and believe me, this has *not* been a good day."

He graced her with a soft smile. "I can tell." Then, gesturing around them at the breathtaking scenery, he said, "Then let me be the first to welcome you to the beautiful Blue Ridge Mountains. We're in a pretty quiet stretch of them, but there are a few small towns nestled in some of the valleys— Chestnut Cove is one of them."

As he was speaking, he'd put the truck in gear, and with a lurch, they were off, rumbling over the same dips in the road and exposed tree roots that Natalie had attempted to navigate earlier. Gabe, though, looked as relaxed as could be, with one hand casually guiding the truck as he leaned back in his seat, chatting easily about the town—it turned out he'd been born and raised in Chestnut Cove, and returned there as an adult. Natalie, still half-frozen, was content to listen to him speak right now, happily wiggling her toes in front of the floor heater in an attempt to thaw them.

After a quick stop at her car so she could grab her suitcase, they soon turned off the main road and navigated a series of paved back roads that Natalie hadn't noticed the first time around. These were mostly plowed, with the snow piled high along the sides of the road, and as they continued descending the mountain, a valley suddenly broke into view among the snowy trees. Natalie released a sigh of relief as the valley spread out before them; by now, she could make out the distinct shapes of buildings and houses, along with an interconnected web of roads.

Life, she thought, nose pressed to the window as the town marched steadily into view. Sweet, glorious, *wonderful* life.

Gabe, who was watching her from the corner of his eye, gave a long, low laugh. "I bet you're pretty relieved to see the town right about now."

"You have no idea." Natalie took a celebratory swig of hot chocolate, grateful that at least *something* had gone right today. She felt another rush of elation in her stomach as they neared the town limits, its green "welcome" sign standing in stark contrast to the snowy surroundings.

Chestnut Cove

Population 1,291

"Enter as strangers, leave as friends"

"What a lovely sentiment," Natalie murmured, then blushed as tears sprang unexpectedly to her eyes. Tears of relief, yes, but tears of something else, too... something that felt an awful lot like longing.

She had never been part of a community, not really, not since the loss of her home and her parents, the loss of her innocence. She'd mainly bounced around since then, never feeling quite like she belonged—until she met Devin, and he offered her the world.

And then ripped it all away.

"You okay?" Gabe was looking at her with soft, searching eyes, and she quickly wiped away the tears with the back of her hand while letting out an embarrassed laugh.

"I'm fine. Just grateful that you found me."

He reached over and gave her knee a quick squeeze, his touch unexpected but not entirely unwelcome. "I'm just glad I decided to go looking for a Christmas tree today," he said. "I saw the weather and almost had a change of plans."

They were in the town proper now, and Natalie gazed around at the cabins tucked into the mountainside, each more cozy than the next. Even though Christmas was still several weeks away, each one of them was fully decorated, the exteriors draped with twinkling lights and lush evergreen wreaths, while the windows were decked with bows and bells and holiday figurines. Not a single cabin was undecorated.

Natalie frowned. Strange. Not a *single* one.

"People sure seem to like Christmas around here," she observed in a casual voice as Gabe took the twisting mountain roads toward the middle of town, which was marked by an enormous bell tower that... yep. It, too, was wrapped with garland and lights and even more bows, and was that a Santa sleigh perched on top? Yes, yes it was, and a feeling of unease was unwinding itself in the pit of Natalie's stomach, and some of the elation she had been experiencing was definitely beginning to evaporate.

Then they reached the town square, and what was left of it evaporated altogether.

Christmas. Christmas here, Christmas there, Christmas *everywhere*.

And oh, the decorations. Santa Clauses wearing red, Santa Clauses wearing gold. Elves with pointy ears, elves with pointy shoes. Wreaths with red bows, silver bows, plaid bows. Garland draped on every imaginable surface. Nutcrackers and snowmen, angels and wise men. Candles and nativity scenes, carolers and reindeer. White lights and colored lights, icicle lights and tree lights.

Everywhere she looked was a literal Christmas explosion. Natalie could feel her heart seizing up, her breath stalling, the blood in her veins turning to ice.

She didn't register that Gabe had parked the truck in front of a beautiful gray stone house until he spread his arms wide and announced, "Welcome to Chestnut Cove." He grinned at her, his eyes bright, his face proud. "The unofficial home of Christmas."

CHAPTER 4

"As you can see, we take the holidays very seriously around here," Gabe said as he swung Natalie's suitcase out of the backseat and set it at her feet. "The townspeople always joke that our blood runs red and green."

Natalie gave him a faint smile as she hitched up the handle on her suitcase and looked around. If she could look past the Christmas explosion, the town square was quite pretty. Beautiful, even, with traditional stone buildings, cobblestone sidewalks, and streets lined with towering trees whose bare branches were dusted with glittering snow. The entire town was ringed by evergreen trees that climbed up the surrounding mountainsides toward the peaks, and the sun shimmering down from the aquamarine sky cast everything in an ethereal glow.

"Why?" Natalie asked, smiling at an elderly couple who greeted her as they walked by, hand-in-hand. "Why the obsession... er, *focus*, on Christmas?" She glanced around for Gabe, then, noticing he had grabbed her suitcase and was wheeling it up the sidewalk toward the gray stone house, she hurried to catch up. The house was stunning, like something out of a fairytale, with white trim and gables, and a trellis draped with ivy and gently twinkling lights. A sign outside proclaimed, in curling, elegant script, *The Mistletoe House.*

"The town was founded in the late 1800s by a family called Holiday, and I guess they decided to lean into the name," Gabe said. He approached the front door, but instead of knocking, he pushed it open, then stood aside to let Natalie enter. "Go on, Faith won't bite," he said with a good-natured chuckle as Natalie hesitated on the threshold.

Before she could make heads or tails of his last words, he continued, "Anyway, because Chestnut Cove is in a relatively isolated spot, the town initially struggled, so the Holidays put their heads together to come up with a way to boost the economy. They decided one year to transform the town into a

Christmas wonderland and invite tourists to visit... and it was such an incredible success that they decided to do it the next year, and the year after that, and then a fourth year."

As he was speaking, he joined Natalie in the home's grand foyer, both of them stamping snow from their boots onto the welcome mat. An ornate front desk stood a few feet away from them across from an enormous Christmas tree decorated with red and gold bows and dozens of strings of lights. Several sets of keys hung on hooks behind the desk, and it occurred to Natalie for the first time that The Mistletoe House wasn't a house at all—it was an inn.

Gabe removed his hat, revealing a full head of thick, dark hair, his brown eyes sparkling appealingly. "And now here we are, more than a hundred years later, and Chestnut Cove has become *the* destination for Christmas-loving folks. We have "Countdown to Christmas" celebrations all year long, we throw a big festival for Christmas in July, and then, of course, we go all out during the month of December." He rang the bell at the desk, then returned his attention to her with a grin. "So you definitely picked the best time of year to get stranded on our mountain."

"I sure did," Natalie said with a weak smile,

turning on her heel in a slow circle to take in her surroundings. The Mistletoe House was the embodiment of Victorian-era style and class, with intricately woven throw rugs, beautiful dark wood embellishments, and rich velvet fabric covering the sofas and armchairs. There were high ceilings, tall windows that let in plenty of light, and a stunning gray brick fireplace beneath a stained-glass mirror. A circular staircase led to the second and third floors, the wall beside it lined with black-and-white photographs. A crystal chandelier hung from the third-floor ceiling, casting glittering shards of light on the floor below.

"This place is incredible," Natalie said, her voice filled with awe. She slid her arms out of her peacoat and hung it on the old-fashioned coatrack beside the front door. "Do you think there's a room available for a couple of nights?" While she wasn't thrilled to be stuck in Christmas town, she had to admit that, Christmas decorations aside, The Mistletoe House would be a charming and comfortable place to stay while her car was being repaired.

"I'm sure Faith can rustle up something for you, especially when she hears what kind of day you had," Gabe said with a soft smile. "Faith is a Holiday, by the way. Great-great-granddaughter of the town's founders, I believe. Ah, here she is now," he added as the sound of footsteps descending the stairs had them both glancing up.

The woman approaching them had beautiful white hair tucked back in a bun, a broad, welcoming smile, and funky square-shaped glasses with purple frames. Her earrings were shaped like Christmas presents, and she wore a glittery red and green sweater with an enormous Santa face plastered across the front. Attire aside, Natalie immediately liked her.

"Gabriel!" Faith Holiday spread her arms wide and immediately pulled Gabe into what looked like a bone-crushing hug. "I haven't seen you in ages, sweetheart. Where have you been hiding?" She pulled back, then looked him over with a critical eye. "Still not eating enough, I see. You need a little meat on those bones." She pinched his arm—his very *muscular* arm, Natalie realized now that he'd removed his own coat. "Tell Holly you need another dozen of her sugar cookies, and this time, don't let Sophie eat them all."

Then the woman turned her attention to Natalie, who was still hovering beside Gabe, feeling slightly awkward. "Well hi there, honey. What brings you to The Mistletoe House?"

"This is Natalie Belmont," Gabe offered, watching in amusement as Natalie offered her hand... only to be pulled into one of Faith's pulverizing hugs instead. "I found her stranded on the side of the road, trying to walk all the way down the mountain wearing those." He nodded toward Natalie's tennis shoes, and Faith clucked sympathetically.

"GPS?" she asked Gabe.

"GPS," he confirmed. "Her car broke down, and I warned her Vernon wouldn't be able to tow it back to town until tomorrow."

"I hope you didn't have anywhere important to be tonight," Faith said, patting Natalie's shoulder. "But in the meantime, let's get you set up in one of the rooms. You're in luck—the snowstorm caused a cancelation, or there would have been no room at the inn."

"No room at the inn," Natalie murmured with a slight shake of her head as she followed Faith to the front desk. Exactly what kind of twilight zone had she entered?

"Here we are, room 3A," Faith said, jangling the room keys merrily. "Follow me, honey, and we'll get you all settled in."

"No elevator?" Natalie asked when she realized Faith was heading for the staircase—the very winding, very steep staircase. She glanced down at her suitcase uncertainly. She'd been in such a rush to leave that she hadn't exactly packed light, throwing half of what she owned inside before storming out of Devin's house.

"Here. Let me." Gabe had been slipping on his coat, preparing to leave, but he stopped what he was doing to hoist Natalie's suitcase into his arms while she followed behind him, stammering her thanks.

"Chestnut Cove hospitality," Faith said as she walked beside Natalie, surprisingly spry for a woman of her age. For her part, Natalie was huffing and puffing by the time they reached the second-floor landing, and was concentrating on successfully reaching the third level without keeling over. Despite that, she couldn't help admiring the ease with which Gabe was climbing the stairs ahead of her, suitcase propped on one shoulder as if it were feather-light.

Faith, noticing this, directed a mischievous wink Natalie's way. "If I were thirty years younger…"

"If *I* were thirty years older," Gabe replied, grinning as he reached the third floor. He set the suitcase at Natalie's feet—she was busy making a horking sound as she tried to catch her breath—and then slid an arm around Faith's shoulders. "I'd be the luckiest guy in town."

"Oh, you." Faith graced him with a flirtatious slap on the arm. "You flatter me, but you know what? There aren't too many men fawning over me anymore, so I'll take it." She made a shooing motion with her hands. "Now go, hero of the mountain, patron saint of stranded travelers. You have many important things to do. I'll take good care of your new friend here."

Natalie, who had been watching their exchange with amusement, turned to Gabe with a warm smile. "Thank you again... so much. You literally saved my life."

"It was my pleasure." Gabe clasped her hand in his, just briefly, just for the space of several heartbeats, but at his touch, Natalie felt something shift in the pit of her stomach. There and gone before she could fully process it, but she quickly removed her hand from his all the same. It had been a long day, she decided. A long, *long* day, and even though it was still mid-afternoon, she was nearly delirious with exhaustion.

"Tell Holly I said hi." Faith waved as Gabe descended the stairs, then she removed the keys to Natalie's room from her pocket and inserted them into the lock. She opened the door just as the inn's front door closed behind Gabe with a distant *thud*, and moments later, they were standing inside, Faith's face lit up with pride as she gestured around the room.

"Gorgeous, isn't it?" the older woman said proudly as she flipped on the light. And while Natalie had to admit that the room was charming and comfortable—or else it *would* be without the many Santa Claus figurines staring back at her, not to mention the tabletop Christmas tree, three wreaths, wooden nativity scene, and illuminated angel—she couldn't stop her heart from sinking into her feet. Faith, watching her closely, frowned. "Is something wrong, dear?"

"No," Natalie said quickly. "No, it's lovely. I'm just... I've had a long day, that's all."

"Say no more." Faith bustled over to the gas fireplace, flipped a switch, and a moment later, red and orange flames were filling the room with gorgeous warmth. Then, after plumping the pillow and folding back the comforter (decorated with dancing elves, Natalie noticed with a wince), she gestured to the bed. "Your nap awaits. If you need anything, just pick up the room phone and dial 1. Otherwise, I'll see you when you come downstairs."

"Thank you," Natalie said gratefully, watching as the other woman departed. Only after she heard footsteps descending the stairs did she pad across the room and quietly close the door. Then she turned, observing the room with a sigh. After squinting at one of the Santa Claus figurines, this one jolly and plump and holding a miniature scroll containing a "naughty" and "nice" list, she shook her head and turned it so that it was facing the wall. Then she did the same with the others, and the angel, too.

"It's only for one night," she reminded herself out loud as she kicked off her shoes and sank onto the plush bed. She could pretend to like Chestnut Cove —and even Christmas—for a single night.

CHAPTER 5

"Oh yeah, you're lookin' at ten days, maybe a coupla weeks," Vernon said, scratching his salt-and-pepper beard as he wiped his hands on an oil-stained rag and closed the hood of Natalie's car with a sigh.

"I'm sorry, did you say a couple of *weeks*? As in fourteen days?" Natalie stared at the mechanic in horror. With Faith's help, she'd given Vernon a call the morning after she'd arrived in town, and by noon, he'd retrieved her car and examined it at his shop. She'd expected him to say a few hours, maybe a single day, tops, but *this*? No way. No sir.

He nodded, then gave his beard another scratch as he waddled ahead of her toward his office, which was overflowing with paperwork to the point that it covered every surface. He settled behind his desk with a groan, his ample stomach straining against the uniform he wore.

"That's if you're lucky," he said, pulling out a clipboard and pen and beginning to take notes. "The engine's busted and I've got to order several new parts. The holidays are right around the corner, and I don't know if you've noticed, but we're not exactly the easiest town to get to. Shipments to Chestnut Cove are slow on a good day, but the weatherman's sayin' more snow is on the way. So if the mountain roads become impassable…" He shrugged. "I wouldn't say the new year isn't outside the realm of possibility."

"The new year?" Natalie spluttered. There was no way, *no way*, she was spending the holidays in Chestnut Cove, home of the world's most annoyingly festive people. She'd probably get dragged to a cookie-baking contest, or a tree-lighting ceremony, or some other such nonsense. Just this morning, she'd stepped out of The Mistletoe House to find carolers howling out Christmas tunes on the sidewalk, smiling cheerfully at everyone who passed.

Natalie may or may not have scowled at them.

"Listen," she said, pressing her hands against Vernon's desk and leaning forward to look him in the eye, "I can't be here for fourteen days. I can't even be here for three days." Her voice was shaking; panic was starting to set in. "I *need* to get out of here. I need to. I'll do whatever it takes, pay whatever it takes…" Her credit card had a little wiggle room left on it, and she still had one last paycheck from Devin to cash before… well, she didn't know what came next, exactly, but she would figure it out, because she always did.

Vernon's smile was kind, but his tone was firm. "Look, if there was any way for me to help you out, speed things along, believe me, I would. But it's just not possible." He sighed and set down the notepad he was holding. "I'll give my parts guy a nudge, see what he can do. But that's the best I can do. No promises, okay?"

"Okay," Natalie said, her heart sinking into her feet at the prospect of another two weeks in this town. "Thank you." After leaving the mechanic her phone number, Natalie headed out of the shop, wandering along the sidewalks with nowhere in particular to be. It was a glorious day, the cerulean sky seeming to stretch to infinity above the surrounding silver-white mountain peaks, a puffy cloud drifting by every so often, its edges high-lighted gold from the sun.

Despite the quaintness of the town, the sidewalks were bustling with people, many of them holding shopping bags overflowing with Christmas decorations, or nursing to-go cups of coffee and hot chocolate, or humming along with the carolers who were still belting out holiday favorites on what seemed like every corner. There were several bell-ringers collecting donations for the less fortunate, and Natalie dropped a few dollar bills into the next collection tin she passed.

"Thank you, miss," the volunteer said, tipping his head at her in gratitude and offering her a sprig of mistletoe in return. She hesitated, then tucked it into the lapel of her peacoat. *When in Rome...* she thought, then slowed her pace as she approached a crowd of people gathered around a window display, many standing on tiptoe to see over the others' shoulders.

She joined them, glancing up at the red and gold awning above the display, then at the sign hanging just below it that read, in old-fashioned script, *Santa's Toy Shop*. The interior of the shop was vast and crammed with toys that whirled, toys that bobbled, toys that lit up, toys that sang...

It was a wonderland, Natalie thought with a smile, trying to imagine how her nine-year-old self would have felt entering a store like that. In the years after the tragedy, her grandmother had done her best to reintroduce some semblance of normalcy into Natalie's life, and they'd even gone through the motions of Christmas: baking cookies, writing letters to Santa, even decorating the tree one year, though that had failed spectacularly, and ended with both of them in tears. Eventually they'd stopped altogether, doing little to mark the day aside from attending the midnight Mass at Grandma's church, something she insisted on.

A woman and child in front of Natalie shifted, giving her a clear view of the window display. She inched closer, her breath frosting the glass as she took in the animated Santa Claus presiding over his elves, who were busy making toys, their little hammers rising and falling rhythmically over their workbenches. Mrs. Claus stood beside her husband, one hand holding a tray of sugar cookies shaped like Christmas trees, the other feeding a reindeer whose tail was wagging in time with the elves' hammers. There was a bright, beautiful Christmas tree in one corner of the display, and a carousel with spinning lights in the other, and...

"Are you okay, dear?"

Natalie turned to find an elderly woman standing beside her looking at her in concern, and only then did she realize her eyes were wet, her cheeks streaked with tears. "I'm fine," she said, quickly patting her cheeks dry as she let out a small, embarrassed laugh. "It's just..." She waved toward the display, and the woman nodded, her eyes warm with understanding.

"Christmas is a magical time, isn't it?" She rested a gloved hand on Natalie's arm. "I still tear up every time I hear 'O Holy Night.' It was my husband's favorite." She gave her arm a gentle squeeze. "Merry Christmas, dear."

"Merry Christmas," Natalie managed, then backed away from the display, slowly at first and then more quickly, and by the time she cleared the crowd, she was practically jogging, her breath escaping in clouds around her. This place... it was getting to her. It was messing with her head, but she had no choice other than to make the best of it until she could hightail it back down the mountain and... what, exactly? No fiancé, no job, no home.

Well. Nothing could be done about the first problem, and the third would come in time... but number two? Number two, she could do something about, starting right now.

After a quick stop at The Mistletoe House to grab her laptop, she headed back out into the cold, making a beeline for The Chestnut Café, an adorable coffee, pastry, and sandwich shop located right next door. She'd grabbed dinner there to go last night, a roasted turkey and cranberry sandwich that had been positively to-die-for, and she was now eager to sample some of the incredible-looking treats behind the display case while she started her job search.

A blast of warmth greeted her as she stepped inside, the jingle bells above the door tinkling pleasantly above her head as a pretty woman about her own age waved to her from behind the counter. "Take a seat anywhere you like," she called, slipping a blueberry muffin into a paper bag for the customer standing beside the cash register. "I'll be there in just a few seconds with a menu."

"Take your time," Natalie called back, slipping off her coat and draping it on the back of her chair. The café was relatively quiet, probably between the lunch and dinner rush, and the only other customers were a middle-aged couple enjoying coffee and sharing a newspaper while holding hands across the table.

Natalie felt a rush of envy as she watched them for a few moments, then, when the woman glanced up, she quickly averted her eyes. The past twenty-four hours had been a blur, not leaving much time for her to dwell on her breakup, but Devin's face popped into her mind just then, the pain sharp and brutal as a knife wound. She wondered what he was doing right now. If he missed her. If he regretted what he had done. If he really was the man she thought he was.

For some strange reason, Gabe's face replaced Devin's in her mind then—his gentle smile, his easy laugh, the respect and concern he'd shown for her, a complete stranger. He'd helped her when she needed help the most. Now *that* was the kind of man every woman deserved.

"Cookie?"

Natalie blinked several times, realized she had been staring vacantly at her laptop screen, and turned abruptly to face the woman standing beside her, the same one who had greeted her from behind the counter. The apron she wore was dusted with flour and smeared with chocolate, and she was holding a tray of sugar cookies shaped like Santa Claus heads, perfectly decorated and incredibly enticing.

"You look like you could use a cookie." The woman smiled at Natalie as she gently lifted a cookie from the tray with a pair of tongs and set it on the plate in front of her. The Santa had rosy icing cheeks and a swirly beard, and Natalie couldn't stop herself from taking an enormous bite, hints of vanilla and almond hitting her tongue as she sighed happily.

"That," she said, "is delicious." She waved toward the display case, which was loaded with freshly baked pies, cakes and cupcakes in various sizes and flavors, and tray upon tray of cookies. "Did you make these?"

"Every last one." The woman's face held just a hint of pride. "I'm Holly Archer. I own the café, which means anytime you come in here, I'll probably be behind the counter." She stuck out her hand and gave Natalie's a shake. "Gossip spreads fast around here, so you don't need to introduce yourself. I already know you're the woman whose car broke down way up on the mountain." She laughed, and Natalie frowned thoughtfully.

"Archer?" she said. "Are you related to—"

The sentence hadn't fully formed when Gabe walked through the door, accompanied by swirls of snow and a little girl with blonde pigtails and cheeks that were bright pink from the cold. "Mommy!" the girl squealed as soon as she laid eyes on Holly, skipping toward her as Gabe followed at a more sedate pace. His eyes warmed when he saw Natalie, and he acknowledged her with a nod before placing his hand on Holly's shoulder and kissing her on the cheek.

Natalie returned his nod with a little wave of her own, then quickly turned her attention back to her laptop screen to give them some privacy, and *where* was that twinge of jealousy coming from? And why, and how, and about a hundred other questions, because she didn't know Gabe, and even if they weren't near-strangers, of course he was married, because why wouldn't he be?

And why did she even care to ask herself these questions in the first place? *That* was the real question... and why had she said the word "question" to herself about a thousand times in the last ten seconds?

Good God. She needed help.

Natalie took another enormous bite of her cookie, just for something to do, and blushed as the table beneath her was showered with crumbs.

"How was she?" Holly asked, neither of them paying attention to Natalie—because why *would* they be?—as she stroked the little girl's hair fondly. "Did the two of you have a good time?"

"We had a wonderful time," Gabe responded, at the exact moment the little girl tugged on Holly's apron and said, "Guess what, Mommy? Guess what?" Her eyes were bright. "We saw Rudolph!"

Holly gasped. "You did! What a wonderful surprise. Did you give him a carrot?"

"No, but she tried to feed him a snowball," Gabe answered with a chuckle. "He wasn't pleased."

As the little girl continued chattering excitedly, Holly slipped a menu onto Natalie's table, whispered, "Give me a shout when you're ready to order," and steered her daughter toward a table by the Christmas tree. A steaming mug of hot cocoa and a cookie followed in short order, and as the girl munched away happily, Gabe and Holly spoke quietly behind the counter. A few moments later, Gabe headed out of the café, waving to Natalie once more before he stepped outside.

Natalie's eyes lingered on his back as he strode down the street, hands tucked deep in the pockets of his coat. When he'd disappeared around a corner, she looked up to find Holly watching her carefully, her expression unreadable. Natalie gave her a quick smile and returned to her work, her cheeks burning with embarrassment at having been caught admiring another woman's husband.

No more of *that*.

Was it time to bury herself in her work before

Holly tore the cookie from her hand and kicked her out into the snow? Yes, sir, it absolutely was.

The job search was tedious and frustrating, and after an hour of tapping away at the keyboard and two cups of coffee, Natalie had only identified two possible opportunities within a one-hour drive of the home she shared with Devin... though she supposed she could expand that radius, because she had no particular place, or city, that she truly called home. Not anymore.

Another hour, and her vision was blurring, not to mention she had polished off a third cup of coffee and was starting to feel jittery. Deciding to call it a day, Natalie snapped her laptop shut and was just debating what to do next when the café's door flew open and Faith Holiday barged in, looking slightly frantic.

"Holly!" the innkeeper shouted, and Natalie could see wisps of white hair escaping from her bun. "Holly!" she called again, her voice rising. "We have an emergency! Jeannie's come down with the flu, and we need an elf."

She turned, looking around for Holly, but her gaze landed on Natalie instead.

And then, to Natalie's horror, the older woman's eyes lit up.

CHAPTER 6

*N*atalie stood from her chair abruptly, shoving her laptop in her bag and her arms in her coat sleeves as fast as she could, doing her best not to make eye contact with the woman now striding toward her with a purpose. She glanced around for a back exit, a hole in the wall, a crack in the floor she could disappear through… anything to avoid whatever idea Faith Holiday seemed to have gotten in her head.

Could she accidentally-on-purpose knock her plate to the floor and cause a scene? Could she faint? Could she find a way to knock herself unconscious —so sorry, Faith!—so she had to be sent to the hospital?

Time was running out, and Faith was still making

a beeline for Natalie, and before she could decide what to do, she felt a firm but polite finger tapping her on the shoulder. Natalie squeezed her eyes shut for a moment, praying she had misheard Faith's original words. Maybe she didn't need an elf at all. Maybe she needed an... elk? Was that any better?

"Natalie, dear." By now, Natalie had no option but to acknowledge Faith's presence, which she did with a smile. A very pained smile. Faith was standing beside her in a Christmas tree sweater, colorful puff balls glued to the fabric to represent ornaments, white fluff on the bottom for the snow. Her eyes were bright, and her smile was a bit mischievous.

Natalie's own smile stretched wide. Now was the time to pretend to faint. And if she actually knocked herself unconscious on the way down? Well... that wouldn't be all bad, would it?

But politeness, hard-drilled into her by her parents, and then her grandmother, won over. So it was with an internal sigh that she said, "Hi, Faith. How's your day?"

"Well, to tell you the truth, it hasn't been so good." Faith's hands were clasped in front of her, and her expression was earnest and filled with hope. Natalie nearly had to look away—it was like staring into the sun.

"Oh?" Natalie managed, hoping to sound both encouraging and yet faintly uninterested. She offered no other words.

Faith, however, was undeterred. "Yes, you see, every year, Chestnut Cove transforms the town hall into Santa's Wonderland—it's our biggest event of the season, and responsible for a huge boost in tourism, which, as you know, helps our economy, which in turn helps small business owners like Holly here."

Holly gave them a merry wave from behind the counter.

"Needless to say, we go all out, but our biggest attraction is our Santa Claus, of course. Walter has been playing the part for thirty-some years now—in fact, he's been our town Santa for so long that he's starting to look the part all year round." She grinned, then her expression immediately turned sober again. "And no Santa Claus is complete without his helper, don't you think?"

Faith gave Natalie an expectant look, clearly awaiting a response. Natalie nodded weakly, one eye still on the exit, which Holly was now blocking as she hung tinsel around the door frame. Was that on purpose? *No*, Natalie decided. Now she was just being paranoid.

Satisfied with Natalie's non-response, Faith continued, "And Jeannie, our elf, has just come down with the flu. I've looked far and wide, and I can't find *any*one to replace her on such short notice." She paused again, and then her voice turned tragic. "And the children, Natalie, they'll be *so* disappointed." She shook her head. "Think of the children."

Natalie swallowed hard. "Um, yes. The children."

Faith clapped her hands once, her eyes lighting up with unmistakable delight. "So you'll do it?"

"Sorry?" Natalie began inching toward the door, then glanced down at her wrist. "Oh, my, look at the time! I actually have an, uh, interview? Yes, an interview for a new job. It's a video call, you see, so I'll just head back to The Mistletoe House and…"

But she trailed off as she saw Faith's gaze following her wrist as she gestured wildly—her bare wrist, because Natalie wasn't actually wearing a watch. Or even owned one, if she wanted to get technical about it. Her face burned as the lie caught up with her, but Faith only smiled sweetly.

"You run along to your interview, dear. Of course, it's perfectly natural that you wouldn't want to be our elf. I'm putting you on the spot. It's just that I've asked everyone I know, and no one can do it." She shook her head forlornly. "The children will understand, of course they will. We'll find someone else to take their picture with Santa, and hand out the treat bags."

She gave Natalie a hopeless look. "That's the part they love the best, you know—the treat bags. Handed to them by one of Santa's real elves! You should see the looks on their faces... and Walter, of course, he and his wife have gone to *such* trouble making them this year. They always do a wonderful job. Such *good* people." Then she sighed heavily. "I'm sure I can find someone else on short notice, someone who doesn't have much to do for the next few days..."

By now, Natalie was only steps from the café's door, with Faith inching along beside her, looking for all the world like someone's adorable grandmother. "I do have to go now," she said, tapping her laptop firmly, "but I'll see you back at the inn later, Faith, okay? And good luck with the, uh, elf search."

Her hand landed on the doorknob, and she was seconds away from freedom when Faith grabbed her arm. "I'll give you a free room at the inn for the rest of your stay if you'll do it."

At this, Natalie paused. A free room? For at least a few days, potentially more than two weeks. Her thoughts roamed to her bank account, which wasn't exactly flush with cash. She had a little put away, sure, but her job at the ice cream shop didn't come with phenomenal pay; she stayed because she loved it, and Devin. And while she still had one last paycheck on the way, she had no idea how long it would take to find another job, not to mention a new place to live. Rent wasn't exactly cheap these days…

"And free breakfast for a week!" Holly chimed in, grinning at Faith. Then she turned to Natalie. "You'd be doing the whole town a favor, and I promise you'll have the time of your life. Besides, you'll have a really good story to tell for years to come."

Natalie hesitated, glancing from one earnest face to the other. The people of Chestnut Cove had been so kind to her, so welcoming, and she definitely owed them several favors… but this? This was a nightmare wrapped in a hefty dose of humiliation, and why was she nodding along? *Why* was she so polite?

"Okay," she heard herself saying. "Sure, I'll do it."

"Oh, thank you!" Faith wrapped her in a suffocating embrace. "Thank you, Natalie, thank you! You won't regret it." Then she pulled back from her with a grin. "Now come with me. We have to make sure the ears are the right fit."

THE EARS WERE MOST DEFINITELY *NOT* the right fit, though Faith didn't seem to agree.

"Oh, Natalie, you look *wonderful!*" she cried, steering Natalie to the mirror in her room at the inn. "Absolutely wonderful! You were born to be Peppermint!"

"Peppermint?" Natalie asked in a weak voice, gently touching the pointy elf ears that Faith had spent the past few minutes showing her how to slip on. They had arrived back at The Mistletoe House and gone directly to Natalie's room, where the elf costume was already waiting on her bed. *"I had a hunch,"* Faith had said with a wink when Natalie pointed this out.

In addition to the prosthetic ears, Peppermint the elf—Natalie's entire body shuddered violently at the name—would be wearing a garish red and green striped dress, glittery tights, a pointed hat with a pom-pom on top, and elf shoes that jingled every time she took a step. She looked ridiculous, positively *ridiculous*, and if anyone actually saw her in this costume, she would die right on the spot.

"Tomorrow is opening day, and we're expecting about a thousand people," Faith said, squinting as she studied Natalie's costume for a moment before shaking her head and heading into the inn's hallway. Natalie heard a closet door opening, then the sound of Faith rummaging around in bags before she reappeared with a sewing kit and several red and green puff balls. Holding the sewing needle between her teeth, she began unwinding thread with expert fingers, then assessed Natalie again before removing the needle and deftly sewing the balls to the hem of the elf dress.

"Did you say a *thousand*?" Natalie asked, torn between horror and wonder. "Can this town even hold that many people?" Everything she'd seen so far had been the epitome of quaint; as far as she could tell, Chestnut Cove didn't have even a single traffic light.

"Oh, you'd be surprised," Faith said, stepping back to examine her work. "There now." She nodded, then gave Natalie a thumbs-up. "I think we're in business."

Which brought up an excellent question, Natalie decided.

"What exactly will I be doing as, er, Peppermint?" she asked, trying not to cringe on that last word and failing at it spectacularly. "What are the job duties of an elf?"

"Oh, the usual things," Faith responded, as if this were a perfectly rational question. "Keeping the line running smoothly, taking photos of the children with Santa, handing out the treat bags." She was ticking off items on her fingers as she spoke. "Answering questions about the town, although I suppose I'll need another volunteer to help with that, since you've only been here a single day. Leading the Santa Claus song, helping—"

"I'm sorry, what was that last one again?" Natalie asked, ice trickling down her veins.

Faith stopped ticking off items with a frown. "Handing out the treat bags?"

"No, after that."

"Answering questions about the town?"

Natalie was beginning to sweat. "No, the part about the song?"

"Oh, that," Faith said merrily. "Well, at the start and end of every session, Peppermint the elf leads the crowd of children and their parents in a fabulous rendition of 'Here Comes Santa Claus.' The singing is sometimes so loud we can hear it on the street." She sighed happily. "It really helps to get everyone in the Christmas spirit. One of the highlights of the day."

Natalie tried to swallow, but her throat felt like sandpaper. "I, um. Can't exactly sing?"

Nails on a chalkboard was too generous for the otherworldly sounds that escaped her anytime she tried to sing. Devin once lovingly described it as a "coyote stuck in a trash compactor."

Natalie was definitely sweating now, which was unbecoming for an elf. "I can't sing," she said, this time more desperately. "Like, at all."

"Oh, that won't be a problem." Faith's voice was relentlessly cheerful, and Natalie had the urge to start tearing puff balls from her costume and throwing them at her. "You just have to sing the first few lines into the microphone, and then the crowd will join in. Believe me, the children will be so excited about seeing the man in red that they won't even notice if you sound like Mariah Carey."

Faith grinned at her, but Natalie was already shaking her head. "No," she said, kicking off one elf shoe, then the other. "No, no no *no*, no no. I'm sorry, Faith, but I'm not cut out for the job." The pointy hat came next, with Natalie tossing it onto the bed in a sad heap. "Not only am I not very good with kids," she said, groping around her back for the zipper to the elf costume, "but I hate Christmas. I actually *hate* it." She stopped what she was doing and met Faith's eyes in the mirror. "I'm sorry, Faith," she repeated, this time in a near-whisper, "but I'm just not the person you think I am."

To her credit, the older woman didn't even blink. Instead, she stepped forward and rested a gentle hand on Natalie's shoulder. "On the contrary, my dear," she murmured with a wink, "I think you're *exactly* the person I think you are."

CHAPTER 7

*T*he next morning, Natalie was in a very bad mood. Her most recent job application was met with an immediate *thanks, but no thanks* from the hiring manager, her cell phone was hit with an emergency weather alert at four a.m., causing her to tumble off the bed in shock, and her elf costume was riding up her…

Well.

Tugging at it viciously, she stomped along the cobblestone sidewalks toward the town hall, jingling all the way, earning a few alarmed stares from passersby that she studiously ignored. *This was a bad idea,* she repeated in her head as a never-ending mantra as she brushed the snowflakes from the sleeve of her elf costume, because of course it was snowing. Of *course* it was. And windy. And cold enough to make her nose hurt the moment she stepped outside. The elf costume did little to ward off the cold, and by the time she arrived at the town hall, she was practically growling at everyone she passed.

Then she tugged open the ornate front doors, and her jaw nearly hit the floor.

The interior of the town hall had been transformed into a glittering winter wonderland, with dozens upon dozens of snow-dusted pine trees lit with soft white lights, clouds of very realistic-looking fake snow artfully arranged around the vast room, and silver and gold decorations adorning the walls and dangling from the ceiling. A beautifully carved throne that sat in the middle of a raised stage was draped in red and green velvet, and a pair of stunning white horses stood serenely in front of an actual sleigh in soft, shimmery shades of silver that looked as though it had been carved from ice.

A red carpet blocked off on either side with green velvet rope was where the children would stand in line for Santa Claus, and a long table was set up beside it, laden with so many trays of exquisitely decorated sugar cookies that Natalie was amazed it hadn't buckled under the weight. At the very back of the room, a few dozen men and women, all wearing elf costumes, were buzzing around three enormous wooden workbenches, and Christmas music was drifting out from hidden speakers.

The pièce de resistance, however, was standing in a pen beside Santa's throne, placidly munching on apples of several different varieties while watching Natalie with liquid brown eyes.

"Hey there, buddy," she said, approaching the reindeer, whose tawny fur looked soft and silky. She reached over the pen and stroked his head; he let out a snort of acknowledgement, but continued gnawing on the apple. Leaning in close, she whispered, "I bet you don't really want to be here either, do you?"

Those liquid eyes continued to watch her, solemn and steady, and Natalie stroked his fur for a few more moments before turning... and running directly into Gabe.

"Whoa. Hey there," Gabe said, catching her by the shoulders with a laugh. "Didn't mean to startle you— I was just coming over to say hello." His gaze wandered over her elf costume, his eyes crinkling in amusement. "I see you and Faith had a little... conversation. She's in charge of the whole event, and every year she ropes me into decorating." He gestured around the room.

"Yeah, well, she can be very convincing." Natalie was fairly certain her cheeks were the same shade of red as her elf hat, and if the earth itself decided to open up at that moment and swallow her whole, she would have accepted her fate wholeheartedly.

Gabe laughed again, and a pool of warmth spread low in her belly. This man, he *did* something to her. Something strange, something she'd never experienced before. It almost felt as if… as if she knew him. As if she had always known him. But that was impossible, of course, because the two of them were strangers.

Holly, she reminded herself. His *wife*.

Suddenly, Gabe's hands were in her hair, and a jolt of electricity so powerful shot through her that her knees were shaking. "Your elf hat," he said, his lips tipped up in a soft smile that did little to quell her racing heart. "It was slipping."

"Thanks," Natalie muttered, stepping away from him, looking every which way but into his eyes. Then, casting her mind around for something else to say, she pointed to the trio of workbenches in the back. "What's going on over there?"

"That's our magical workshop," Gabe said, leading her across the room, talking as they walked shoulder-

to-shoulder. "Every fall, we put out a call for toy donations in Chestnut Cove and the surrounding communities. The donations are dropped off here at the town
hall, and every year during our Santa's Wonderland
event, volunteers in elf costumes wrap the gifts and
load them into the sleigh. On Christmas Eve, they
deliver them to children whose parents might not
have the money to buy gifts for them otherwise."

He gave her a crooked smile that was like a bullet
to her heart. "So the magic is twofold: the kids who
come here to see Santa think they're in his actual
workshop, and we do our part in helping to spread a
little extra Christmas cheer."

Tears sprang unexpectedly to Natalie's eyes.
"That's nice, Gabe," she said, hurriedly wiping them
away. "That's really nice."

"Thanks." He gave her a soft smile. "It's all about
community, right? Especially at this time of year.
That's one of the reasons I love Christmas so much
—the togetherness, the sense of belonging. It really
makes me feel like I have a purpose in life."

Natalie didn't respond to that. She couldn't, not
only because she hadn't experienced that in many,
many years, but also because her voice was no
longer working. She looked up to find Gabe

watching her, his eyes intense, probing, as if he could read her thoughts.

Swallowing hard, throat bobbing, she said, "I'd better go. I should probably figure out what I'm supposed to be doing."

"Right." Gabe tore his gaze from hers. He glanced around, then pointed toward the workbenches. "There's Faith. I'm sure she'll be able to tell you exactly what to do."

Natalie gave him a faint smile. "I'm sure she will." Then, with a goodbye nod, she left his side, feeling slightly off-kilter as she headed toward Faith, who was putting the finishing touches on a beautifully wrapped present. Natalie noticed that she wasn't wearing an elf costume, just another entry in the "world's most ridiculous Christmas sweater" contest that she seemed to be participating in on a daily basis. Today's sweater featured a Rudolph made entirely out of... yep. Brown puff balls.

"Natalie! You made it!" Faith sing-songed, as if Natalie had any other choice in the matter. She set the present she was wrapping aside, gave a few quick instructions to a pair of elves on when to begin loading the heaps of wrapped gifts into the sleigh, then took Natalie by the arm and led her toward the stage. "Walter's getting dressed right now, so you'll have a chance to meet him before the festivities begin. The doors open in..." She glanced at her watch. "Goodness! Only half an hour to go. We'd better pick up the pace."

She sped her walk up to a trot, with Natalie hurrying to catch up as Faith gave her a rapid-fire list of instructions, barely pausing to take a breath. She finished with, "...and when you're leading the first verse of 'Here Comes Santa Claus,' make sure you're singing directly into the microphone so the children in the back can hear you." She looked at Natalie. "Did you get all that?"

"I... think so?"

They had reached the stage now, just as Santa Claus waddled out from the men's bathroom.

"Ho, ho, ho, *Merry* Christmas!" he called, waving to the elves still clustered around piles of wrapping paper, ribbons, and bows. "Ho, ho—well, hello there!" Reaching Natalie, he gave her a jolly wave.

"Natalie Belmont, this is Walter Miller," Faith said, making the introductions. "Chestnut Cove's Santa Claus for the past... what is it now, Walt? Thirty-seven years?"

"Thirty-eight," he replied, wagging a finger. Then he stuck out his hand. "Nice to meet you, Natalie. I take it you're our newest elf?"

"In the flesh," Natalie replied with a little curtsy. She couldn't help the grin spreading across her face as she scanned the older man from head to toe. "You're… wow. The most realistic-looking Santa Claus I've ever seen. No wonder so many kids come to Chestnut Cove to see you."

"I try." Walter spread his arms wide, his blue eyes twinkling merrily, his cheeks tomato-red… probably from the heat, Natalie decided, because that Santa suit looked like it weighed about a hundred pounds. His black boots were polished to a proper shine, his belt strained against his ample—*very* ample—belly, and Natalie resisted the urge to tug his long white beard to see if it was real.

"It is," Walter said with a wink, reading her thoughts. "And much to the delight of the missus here, I've recently decided to keep it all year round."

"I'm not sure I'd go *that* far, but I do admit that it suits you." An older woman dressed as Mrs. Claus had approached them and was now standing on tiptoe to kiss Walter on the cheek. "Hello, I'm Carol Miller," she said warmly to Natalie. "I'm so glad you were able to join us today. Thank you so much for helping out. Faith said you would be the perfect elf, and judging by the costume alone, I'd say she's right. You look adorable, dear. Absolutely adorable."

"Thanks," Natalie muttered, shuffling awkwardly in her elf shoes, wincing with every jingle. She still felt ridiculous, though slightly less so, she decided, now that she was here. "I was sorry to hear that Jeannie came down with the flu."

"Jeannie came down with the flu?" Carol frowned, then glanced at Faith, who was nodding vigorously.

"Oh, yes, a terrible flu. Stomach, in fact. Vomit everywhere." Faith mimed throwing up, then shook her head sadly. "It was sort of like watching Mount Vesuvius erupting, the poor thing. But Natalie here was only too happy to help."

Well. She wouldn't go *that* far, but Natalie did have to admit that her foul mood was slipping away, bit by bit. It was hard to be a scrooge in a place like this.

Carol was still giving Faith an odd look. Then she turned back to Natalie. "Well, whatever the reason, I'm glad you're here. If you have any questions, I'll be passing out the cookies." She nodded toward the cookie tables; Natalie could see that the reindeer, having finished his apples, was now eyeing them greedily. He let out a snort and pawed at the hay strewn around the floor at his feet, then pressed his body against the pen, moving it an inch to the side.

Natalie opened her mouth to point this out, but was distracted by a commotion just outside the front doors. Screeches of excitement and cheers of happiness, courtesy of the group of young kids who had just arrived, faces pink from the cold, and spotted Walter standing in full Santa regalia beside his throne.

"Ho, ho, ho," he called to them, opening his arms wide in a welcoming gesture. "Come in, children, come in." Then he turned to Natalie and Faith with a brilliant smile, one that exuded pure joy, a feeling Natalie herself hadn't experienced much of lately. "Ladies and elves, it's showtime."

CHAPTER 8

*B*eing an elf wasn't so bad, Natalie had decided an hour later as she made a silly face behind the camera, hoping to elicit a smile from the little boy now screaming bloody murder on Santa's lap. Yes, she'd sounded like a cat whose tail had been lit on fire during her rousing rendition of "Here Comes Santa Claus," and yes, she had been hacked on twelve times, spit in the face twice, and was now enduring the elf-costume-induced wedgie to end all wedgies, but she'd had worse jobs. And infinitely worse days.

"Come on now, Caleb, give Santa a little smile," Natalie called to the still-shrieking toddler, who could probably be heard at the International Space Station by now. She pressed her eye to the camera lens, then said, "One, two, three... say Christmas cookies!"

Another snort from the reindeer at that last word, and was it Natalie's imagination, or was he much, much closer to the cookie table than he had been fifteen minutes ago?

"C-C-Christmas cookies!" the boy managed to choke out between wails, and Natalie pulled her attention back to the task at hand, snapping the photo with a flourish and gracing the boy's harried-looking mother with a sympathetic smile.

"I think I got it," she said, then waited while the Polaroid shot printed out. The boy's face was contorted in a hideous expression, and Walter, admittedly, looked a bit shell-shocked in the photo, but hey, at least he'd signed up for this willingly, right?

"Merry Christmas," Natalie said to the mother, presenting her with the photo while trying not to laugh. The woman looked at it and grinned, then gathered her son into her arms and carried him, still screaming, toward the exit. Natalie intervened just long enough to hand him a treat bag, then turned to the next child in line. As she did, she noticed Gabe entering the town hall, his dark hair dusted with snow, a red and green plaid scarf wrapped around his neck. He was holding hands with the same little blonde girl she'd seen the day before at The Chestnut Café; the girl was talking animatedly and pointing at Walter, her face wild with excitement.

Natalie's heart sank as she saw the look of love on Gabe's face as he hugged his daughter to his side, just a little—the tiniest bit, really, and who could blame her? Every woman loved a man who adored his daughter, and Natalie felt a sharp pang of jealousy as they entered the line, still holding hands, because she had always envisioned herself as part of a happy little family someday.

Gabe glanced up then, directly into Natalie's eyes, and she mustered up a grin and an enthusiastic wave in the hopes of covering up the humiliating fact that she had been watching him. Over the next fifteen minutes, as Gabe and his daughter marched steadily closer to the front of the line, Natalie performed her elf duties the best she could while sneaking them covert glances... although why, she couldn't quite put her finger on. Maybe she'd hoped that she and Devin would soon have a child of their own. Maybe she was just feeling lonely.

Maybe...

Well. Maybe not.

"And what would *you* like for Christmas, my

dear?" Natalie vaguely heard Walter asking in the background, followed by the sound of him clearing his throat, loudly and pointedly. She jumped and, blushing, grabbed the camera off the table beside her, waiting patiently as the girl on his lap rattled off a list of toys she hoped to unwrap on Christmas day. When she was finished, and Natalie had taken her picture, Walter threw her a look that plainly said, *Are you okay?*

She nodded, her cheeks still on fire, and studiously ignored Gabe for the next few minutes as she threw herself wholeheartedly into her elf duties. Then, just as he and his daughter approached the velvet rope separating Walter from the crowd, an almighty crash shook the entire town hall, followed by a shriek of surprise.

Natalie whipped around just in time to see the reindeer free himself from his toppled-over pen and gallop toward Carol, his liquid eyes laser-focused on the cookies in front of her. Natalie acted without thinking, sprinting toward the charging reindeer, her shoes jingling madly as she cried, "Stop, *stop!*" at the top of her lungs. Children were screaming, parents were shouting, and "Grandma Got Run Over by a Reindeer" was somehow blaring from the overhead speakers as Carol ducked behind the tables just before the reindeer careened into them at full force, Natalie on his heels.

What she was planning to do, she didn't know. But she *did* know one thing.

As soon as she caught up with the reindeer and made a grab for his tail, she saw only the fiery look in his eyes... and the bottom half of his hoof as he thrust it as hard as he could into her ribcage.

Then, darkness.

THE FLUORESCENT LIGHTS above her head were blinding as Natalie blinked once, then twice, then shot up only to fall back again, howling in pain.

"You probably shouldn't do that again."

She was definitely hallucinating, because she could have sworn she heard Gabe's voice. This was followed in short order by his head swimming into view, the smile on his lips one of faint amusement. She tried to sit up again, but this time, a gentle hand pressed her back down.

"Seriously, Natalie, you need to take it easy." Another smile, followed by a chuckle. "Has anyone ever told you that you're a terrible patient?"

"Where am I? What's going on?" Natalie frowned

up at him, then turned her head slowly to take in her surroundings. A blood pressure machine was visible on one side of her, a cabinet full of medical supplies on the other. A tabletop Christmas tree twinkled merrily from one corner of the room, and the sight of the colored lights and baubles brought the memories of the past few minutes flooding back.

Peppermint the elf holding a camera one second, Peppermint the elf sprawled on the floor the next.

"Ugh..." Natalie pressed a hand to her temple, which was thumping with the beginnings of an epic headache. "I don't feel so good."

"No, I should say not." Gabe shined a penlight in her eye, examining her pupils. "The good news is you don't seem to have a concussion, although time will tell on that front. Want to tell me what you remember happening?"

Natalie's mouth was dry and cottony, and she had to swallow several times before she could speak. Gabe, seeing this, rummaged around in the cabinet behind him before producing a bottle of water, twisting off the cap, and passing it to her. She gave him a grateful smile, then chugged half the bottle while her mind tried to slot the jumbled puzzle pieces into place.

"I was running..." she said. "Toward a cookie

table, trying to save Carol Miller from being eaten, and I got kicked in the stomach by an angry reindeer."

Gabe grinned at her. "Mostly true. Humphrey never would have eaten Carol because reindeer are herbivores. And I don't think he was angry—I think he was hungry."

"Humphrey? Please tell me that beast isn't named Humphrey, because that's just ridiculous." Natalie squinted up at the man hovering over her—the very handsome man, she noticed, not for the first time, taking in his dark hair and eyes, and the not-insignificant muscles visible beneath his doctor's coat.

Wait... doctor's coat?

"Are you a doctor?" she asked, realization dawning as she looked around the room. She seemed to be in an office or small hospital of some kind, and surely they didn't let just anyone examine the patients. Of course, Gabe could examine her anytime, from head to toe and all the places in between, and oh, sweet baby Jesus, did she just say that out loud?

She peered at him, trying to determine whether she had, but his face remained smooth and professional, with the exception of the amused glint in his dark eyes.

Crap on a *stick*.

"One question at a time," he said, a smile in his voice. "Yes, that beast is indeed named Humphrey, and he's been a beloved part of Chestnut Cove's Christmas festivities for several years now. He's usually quite the gentleman, but I guess Holly's sugar cookies were too much for him to handle." He clicked the penlight off and slid it back into the pocket of his white coat. "And yes, I am a doctor. The town's only doctor, in fact." He gestured around the room. "Fortunately my office is right next door to the town hall, so Walter and I were able to carry you here." He laughed. "Now those kids think that Santa is not only magical, but he's a hero too."

Leaning forward, he clasped his hands loosely in front of him, his eyebrows furrowed with concern. "How are you feeling?"

"Okay, I guess." She began gingerly pressing her fingers into her body. "My head hurts... a lot." The breath rushed from her lungs in a pained *whoosh* as she got to her chest. "Ouch," she said, wincing.

"May I?" Gabe was standing over her now, hands hovering above her chest. She nodded, feeling self-conscious but trying not to yelp out loud as he tenderly prodded her ribs. "Nothing feels fractured," he murmured, continuing to press gently while she looked every which way but into his eyes. This was awkward. Seriously, seriously awkward, mostly because Natalie was well aware that she'd been having... thoughts... about this man. This very married, very off-limits man.

"While I think you're mostly just going to have some bumps and bruises, I do think we should run a few tests," Gabe said, withdrawing his hands and taking a seat behind his computer to tap out a few notes on the keyboard. "X-ray for the ribs to ensure there aren't any fractures, possibly a CT scan for the head... you hit it off the table on the way down, which is why you passed out, and also why you feel like your head has been trampled by a herd of stampeding reindeer." She cringed, and he laughed. "Too soon?"

"Too soon," she acknowledged. "I'll never look at Rudolph the same way again." She lay back on the exam table with a sigh, then glanced around Gabe's office. "Are you going to be performing the tests here?"

"Unfortunately, we aren't that sophisticated." He pushed back from his computer with a smile. "There's a hospital about thirty minutes from here.

I'll give them a call to let them know we're on our way."

"We?" Natalie asked, attempting to sit up once more. This time she was successful, though the room was still spinning slightly, like she'd just stepped off an amusement park ride. "Are you taking me?"

"You don't have a car, and while we do share an ambulance with a few of the other mountain communities, we try our best to save it for true emergencies." Gabe held out a hand. When she took it, he gave her a soft tug until she was on her feet. "You okay?" he asked, scanning her, his eyes warm with concern.

Her gaze met his, and she nodded. Then he offered her his arm, and she shuffled beside him through the small office and out the back door, where his pickup truck was parked. "I figured we shouldn't go through the front and make a scene," he said, helping her into the passenger seat, his breath clouding around him in the frosty air as he reached around her to buckle her in. Then, with a wink, he added, "And I'm guessing we've already traumatized the children enough for one day."

"Sorry about that," Natalie said, her eyes drifting closed as she settled back against the seat. The snow was still swirling gently outside, the air redolent with the fresh, clean scent of pine and winter, but inside the truck it was cozy and warm. Too cozy, because she could feel herself drifting off again, her thoughts floating in different directions as the warmth enveloped her. "And sorry about your daughter," she murmured as he slid behind the wheel and cranked the engine. "I hope she still gets to visit with Santa…"

Gabe must have responded, because the low rumble of his voice washed over her. But what he said was a mystery, because by the time he finished his sentence, Natalie was already fast asleep.

"THANKS again for chauffeuring me around all day," Natalie said as she and Gabe stood in front of The Mistletoe House later that evening. Twilight had fallen over the mountains, and the mauve sky was streaked with strands of coral and grapefruit from the setting sun. The snow had finally stopped falling, though the cobblestone sidewalks were dusted with white and the trees surrounding them were glittering in the waning light. She had to admit, it was beautiful.

"It was my pleasure," Gabe said. He blew into

his bare hands to warm them from the cold. Carolers were singing on a nearby corner, their voices drifting over the evening air. "I'm just glad you're okay." He smiled at her, his dark eyes dancing with amusement. "I take it no more elf duty?"

"Wrong," Natalie said, surprising even herself. Then, shrugging, she laughed. "Peppermint doesn't hang up her ears that easily. And besides, I'm stuck in this town for another few days, so I might as well have something to do." Gabe's smile flickered at the edges, and she winced. "I'm sorry, that came out wrong," she said, shaking her head. "Chestnut Cove is a lovely town—really, it is. And you and Faith and Walter—and everyone, really—have been so kind to me. But…"

She hesitated, unable to vocalize her feelings. Behind Gabe, the bell in the town square began to ring, signaling the start of a new hour. She recognized the melody of "O Christmas Tree," and her stomach lurched.

Gabe lifted his hands, palms out. "Hey, I get it. No explanations needed, and no offense taken. This isn't your home."

No, it wasn't. Nor was anywhere else.

Natalie swallowed hard, looked at the ground,

tried not to cry. Useless, because her eyes were already burning, but Gabe didn't need to know that.

"Natalie?" he asked softly. She sensed him taking a step toward her, close enough to touch.

"Ouch," she said, pressing her fingers to her temples, feigning a headache. "Sorry, I'm just... I'm really tired." She wiped her eyes as discreetly as she could, then chanced a glance up at him. He was watching her, his gaze on her face, a brand burning into her skin. Their eyes lingered on each other for the space of several heartbeats, and Natalie was first to break the connection.

Because that's what it was. A connection. Undeniable, and impossible.

"I should go." She wiped her eyes again; her cheeks were wet with tears. "Thank you again for your kindness. You have no idea what it means to me."

She turned to leave, and was just about to open the door to The Mistletoe House when a hand pressed against it, stopping her from entering. Glancing over her shoulder, Natalie saw Gabe with his hand on the door, his eyes still locked on hers. "Come with me to the Christmas tree lighting ceremony tomorrow night." His smile was soft. "Please."

She hesitated. The bell was still chiming behind

her, the town was awash in golden light, and this moment could have been perfect. In another life, with another man.

She started to shake her head, but he held his ground. "It's a big deal here in town—our way of officially ringing in the Christmas season. There will be food trucks, a hot chocolate station, maybe a visit from the man in red..." He chuckled. "Although I'm guessing you've seen enough of him today to last a lifetime." He cocked his head at her, his eyes still assessing her face. "Say you'll think about it."

"Sorry." She shook her head again, this time more insistently. "I'm just not... into Christmas, I guess you could say. It's not really my thing." Turning once more, she added, "But I hope you, Holly, and Sophie have a really nice time."

She had one foot in the inn's door when Gabe called out to her, and this time, his words stopped her in her tracks.

"Holly isn't my wife."

Natalie pivoted on her heel slowly to face him. His dark eyes were dusted with copper in the last rays of the dying sun, and a smile was playing across his lips. "She's not my girlfriend, either." His eyes were steady on her face. For some reason, she couldn't breathe.

"Oh?" she managed.

He shook his head. "She's my sister. And Sophie is my niece. Her father isn't in the picture all that much, so I step in where I can." He shrugged. "I'm kind of awesome like that."

At that, Natalie laughed, loud and long. "You *are* awesome like that."

He grinned at her, hands shoved in the pockets of his coats, twinkle lights highlighting his hair with streaks of gold. "So the tree lighting ceremony. You'll consider it?"

A pause. Then, "I'll consider it."

His expression was soft. Hopeful, even. "Goodnight, Natalie."

"Goodnight, Gabe."

This time when she turned to leave, she was smiling.

CHAPTER 9

"*I* heard you spent a little one-on-one time with Gabe Archer yesterday."

Natalie glanced up from the pile of wrapped presents she was helping to load into the sleigh to find Faith Holiday standing beside her with a sly smile. "Lucky woman," she added, nudging Natalie in the side.

The last child had just left Santa's Wonderland, leaving the volunteers to tidy up the town hall and prepare for the next day's festivities. True to her word, Natalie had made her triumphant return as Peppermint the elf to an embarrassingly loud round of applause; apparently, news about her near-fatal encounter with Humphrey had spread through the town like wildfire. She'd made it a point to steer clear of the beast, though she did notice Carol feeding him several sugar cookies over the side of his pen in an obvious attempt to appease him.

"Would you call two X-rays and a CT scan lucky?" Natalie asked, sidestepping Faith's touch with a wince. Her ribs were still smarting from where they'd met Humphrey's hind kick, but other than that, and a hoof-shaped bruise on her side, she had made a full recovery.

Faith shrugged. "I'd call it lucky if that man didn't leave *my* side the entire time." She glanced over to where Gabe was balanced precariously on a rickety-looking ladder beside a Christmas tree, trying to fix a broken bulb on its star. Natalie hadn't had much contact with him today other than a quick exchange of pleasantries; truth be told, she wasn't quite sure how to act around him. That electricity in the air every time they were in close proximity… she wasn't imagining it, and had no idea how to unpack its meaning.

"He's a good man, you know." Faith's eyes were still on Gabe. "A wonderful man, in fact."

"Well, I hear he's available, if you're interested," Natalie said lightly, ignoring the twist of… something… in the pit of her stomach. Something that felt entirely too close to longing. Which was ridiculous, of course, because not only had she just gotten out of a relationship—and not even by choice—but she barely knew him.

She loaded the last of the presents, then stepped back to admire her handiwork. The sleigh was nearly filled to the brim, with several weeks of donations still to go. It was going to be a wonderful Christmas for the children who may not have otherwise had one, and Natalie's heart warmed as she imagined their faces when they woke on Christmas morning.

"Honey, if I were thirty years younger, I would have snapped him up the second he became available," Faith said with a laugh. "It's too bad that good men are so hard to come by."

"What's his story, anyway?" Natalie asked in a would-be nonchalant voice. "Was he ever married?"

Faith paused. "No. He came close, though." She watched Gabe work for a few moments, then glanced at her watch. "We'd better call it a night if we're going to make it to the tree lighting ceremony." Natalie had wanted to know more about Gabe's past, but she sensed that the discussion was closed. Instead, she merely nodded and followed Faith to the door. "You're coming, I hope?" Faith asked as they walked together. "It's a wonderful event. A

Chestnut Cove tradition dating back almost a hundred years."

"I'm not sure yet," Natalie admitted. She'd endured a sleepless night tossing and turning while she considered Gabe's offer, and when the first rays of light finally met her scratchy eyes, she still hadn't come up with an answer. It was... complicated. To say the least.

"Well, for what it's worth, I think you should come." Faith held open the door, and the two women stepped into the blustery evening air. "How's the car coming along?" she asked. "Any word from Vernon?"

Natalie paused. "To tell you the truth, I haven't thought about it." She laughed. "I've been having too much fun as an elf. Minus the whole Humphrey incident, of course." Natalie was surprised by her own words. Somewhere along the way, though, they had become true.

"Of course," Faith said. Then she gave Natalie a mysterious smile. "I can't say I'm surprised to hear that, though. That's the magic of Chestnut Cove."

They were strolling along the sidewalk, and were approaching two little girls accompanied by their parents, all of them exclaiming over the window display at the toy store. The girls, seeing Natalie in full elf costume, let out identical squeals of delight before launching themselves into her arms. A grinning Natalie returned the hug, her eyes tearing up unexpectedly. Faith pulled two candy canes from her purse and passed them to the girls, and the six of them exchanged holiday greetings before going their separate ways.

"What's the magic of Chestnut Cove?" Natalie asked, removing her elf hat to dab at her eyes as Faith watched her with a knowing look. They had reached The Mistletoe House, which was softly lit by the wreaths dangling from every window. It was a welcome sight, and an odd feeling came over Natalie as she took in the beautiful gray stone inn. Despite having stayed there for only a few nights, to Natalie, it was beginning to feel like home.

The women stepped inside and used the welcome mat to stomp the snow off their boots. Before Faith could answer Natalie's question, the phone at the inn's front desk rang. After shrugging out of her coat, Faith took the call. "The Mistletoe Inn, this is Faith. Merry Christmas! Can you please hold?" Then she lowered the receiver and pressed her hand to muffle the sound of her voice as she addressed Natalie instead. "The magic of Chestnut Cove is simple, and beautiful: once you're here, you never want to leave."

As DARKNESS FELL over the mountains, Natalie joined the excited crowd streaming toward the town square, which was ablaze with thousands of twinkle lights strung overhead. The night air was filled with the joyful harmonies of carolers as they sang beloved Christmas songs from a stage that had been erected beside a magnificent pine tree so tall it seemed to scrape the sky. The heady aroma of hot chocolate and cinnamon rolls lingered in the air, and the sidewalks were lined with local vendors selling handmade snow globes, glass ornaments, wreaths, and other holiday wares.

Natalie felt self-conscious as she wandered through the throngs of people, searching for anyone she knew, smiling and nodding in response to the Christmas greetings being delivered her way. Then she rounded a corner and spotted Gabe amid the crowd, his dark hair gleaming beneath the twinkle lights, his shoulders strong and proud, and butter-flies took flight in her stomach, beating their wings in time to the fluttering of her heart.

"Hey, you made it!" Gabe's smile was startling in its beauty as he turned to greet her after she tapped him nervously on the shoulder. He was standing beside Holly and her little girl; both of them waved to her, their faces nearly obscured by the thick Christmas scarves they wore. Sophie was practically bouncing up and down, her pink face shining with excitement, one hand clutching a to-go cup of hot chocolate that smelled positively heavenly.

Natalie's nose took an automatic whiff and, seeing this, Gabe handed her a cup of her own. "I got it just in case," he said, bending low to murmur in her ear as the crowd buzzed around them. Then, without warning, he slid his hand into hers and gave her fingers a soft squeeze. "I was hoping you would come."

His gaze met Natalie's and the world dropped away; in that moment, there was just the two of them, right here, right now. Natalie's heart was a drumbeat in her ears as Gabe stepped closer, his brown eyes sparkling in the moonlight as they roamed over her face, darkening slightly as they lingered on her mouth.

Natalie couldn't breathe. She couldn't *breathe*, and she found herself moving closer to him, the action instinctual... and maybe fated. Then a little girl trilled, "Look, Uncle Gabe, look! Santa Claus is here!" And the moment was broken by Sophie tugging enthusiastically on Gabe's sleeve while Holly tried in vain to shoo her away.

Sorry, she mouthed to Holly with a sheepish smile as Gabe and Natalie jumped apart. Guilt was scrawled all over his face, embarrassment too, and maybe just a hint of annoyance? Probably, because that same trio of emotions was now washing over Natalie, along with a healthy dose of regret.

Not because they'd almost kissed. Because they hadn't.

Still, Natalie would have been hard-pressed to keep the grin from her face as she turned her attention to the unlit tree, where Walter Miller was in his element. He was *ho-ho-hoing* and tossing candy canes into the crowd, much to the delight of the hundreds of children present. His belly was wobbling, his boots were clicking against the pavement, and his beard was glittering with the snowflakes that had begun gently falling. Carol caught Natalie's eye through the crowd and waved energetically before she returned her attention to her husband, her gaze warm with adoration.

How beautiful, Natalie thought, watching them. How wonderful to have found someone to walk through life with. Natalie's own parents had been in love; it was obvious in their every interaction, even at her young age. She wondered if they would have grown old together, if given the chance.

Memories came rushing back to her then, *ping-ping-ping*, each one an arrow penetrating her heart. Natalie and her parents constructing a gingerbread house, the two of them howling with laughter as she leaned forward and licked the icing from the rooftop, smearing it all over her chin. Her mother dancing around the kitchen as she and Natalie baked Christmas cookies, her apron smeared with flour, humming along to Bing Crosby on the old record player. Decorating the tree each Christmas Eve, Natalie reverently unwrapping the keepsake ornament her mother had carefully chosen at the local card shop, her father telling corny jokes as he untangled strands of lights.

No. No, no, *no*, it was too much, all of it.

Natalie sensed Gabe watching her, knew her face was whiter than the snow falling around them, but quickly gave him a smile and feigned a shiver, pulling her peacoat tighter around herself. If she had to stay in town much longer, she'd probably need to invest in some heavier outerwear; most of Chestnut Cove's citizens looked like they were preparing for a trip to the Arctic.

"Cold?" Gabe asked. She nodded, and he moved

behind her. After a moment's hesitation, he tenta-
tively wrapped his arms around her waist, and she
responded by leaning into him, her head against his
chest, barely daring to breathe as their breath
mingled in the icy air. Strange, she noted, how every
time she was in Gabe's presence, all thoughts of
Devin seemed to melt away. In fact, over the past
couple of days, he'd barely crossed her mind...
which was even stranger, given the fact that they'd
been together for more than half a decade.

Maybe she was unconsciously suppressing her
pain, her heartache. Or maybe...

A small orchestra, each musician bundled up
against the cold, slipped into their seats beside the
stage then, and soon the haunting notes of "What
Child Is This" lifted into the night air. Natalie
found herself humming along as she nestled closer
to Gabe, reveling in the feel of his arms around
her, the rightness of this moment despite how
difficult it was for her. This had been her mother's
favorite song, and Natalie clearly recalled her beautiful voice filling the rooms of their home every
time it started to play. She hadn't listened to this
song in years. She hadn't been able to. But
tonight... well, tonight, for the first time in thirty
years, she felt something other than the pure, raw

grief that lurked around every corner during the holidays.

She felt the tiniest flicker of joy.

When the song was over, a silver-haired woman wearing a stylish winter coat and a Santa Claus hat approached the microphone. After tapping it once, she leaned in and called out, "Good evening, Chestnut Cove!"

A round of raucous applause and cheers greeted her, and she waited until the crowd had settled down again to continue speaking.

"For those of you who don't know me, my name is Marina Hartford, and I'm the mayor of this beautiful town. It's my honor to welcome everyone to our ninety-first tree lighting celebration!" Another round of applause from the crowd, and Natalie found herself enthusiastically clapping along.

"As you may know, every year our townspeople nominate one of our citizens to have the honor of lighting the tree. We choose someone who exemplifies the spirit of Christmas, someone who gives back to others, someone who works tirelessly to make our beautiful little town the best it can be. The winner of this year's vote is one of our most beloved citizens. Not only did he develop a traveling clinic to provide medical care to those who are either experiencing financial hardship or are homebound, but he is a leader in our local chapter of Habitat for Humanity, and is on the board of directors for our elementary and middle schools."

Marina's smile was bright as she scanned the crowd. "He is an exemplary man, and a wonderful friend to our community. Without him, Chestnut Cove's light would shine a little less brightly each day. So without further ado, it is my great privilege to welcome Dr. Gabriel Archer to the stage."

Natalie was stunned for a moment as those around her turned to congratulate Gabe with handshakes and cheers. Holly gave him a high-five, and Sophie threw herself at his legs, wrapping him in a long hug that he crouched down to return. As he stood, his gaze snagged on Natalie's, and once again, everything around them faded away, a blur of color and noise that blended into the background.

Congratulations, she mouthed to him, and he grinned at her, his dark eyes shimmering in the moonlight. Then his gaze strayed to her lips again, and her lungs constricted to the size of pinholes as he leaned toward her.

"Come on now, Gabe, don't be shy!" the mayor called out in a sing-song voice. She shielded her eyes with one hand as she scanned the crowd. "I promise

I won't make you sing 'Rudolph the Red-Nosed Reindeer' like we did to Walter last year."

A rumble of laughter rippled through the crowd, and the connection was broken. Gabe reached for her hand and gave it a brief squeeze, a gentle promise of more to come, and then he began working his way through the crowd, which parted to let him through. When he reached the stage, the mayor stepped back from the microphone, gesturing for him to take her place.

"Uh, hi, everyone," he said, lifting his hand and giving the crowd a sheepish wave. "While I'm incredibly honored to light the tree this year, I have to say that Marina made me sound far cooler than I actually am." He raked one hand through his hair, looking adorably awkward. "In reality, I'm just a normal guy who loves his community. Moving back to Chestnut Cove was the best decision of my life, and I'm grateful to share that life with all of you. So thank you, from the bottom of my heart." He moved away from the podium, then leaned in again and added, "Merry Christmas, everyone. And Happy New Year."

The crowd returned his well wishes, then Gabe and the mayor moved to a complicated-looking bundle of wires and equipment beside the stage. She handed him a remote control, then cupped her hands over her mouth and shouted, "Ten, nine, eight…"

Natalie and the rest of the crowd joined in on the countdown, and when they reached "one," the Christmas tree burst into a dazzling array of colored lights as the choir delivered an energetic rendition of "Rockin' Around The Christmas Tree." Styrofoam cups of hot chocolate were raised in the air as people whooped and cheered, and as the song ended and the orchestra played the first notes to a slow, haunting rendition of "Silent Night," hundreds of voices joined in. By the end, tears were streaming down Natalie's cheeks, and this time, she didn't bother trying to wipe them away.

THE SKY WAS midnight black as Natalie finally arrived back at The Mistletoe House, with Gabe waiting in the foyer until she'd climbed the winding staircase to her third-floor room. Only when she'd slotted the key in the lock did she hear the inn's front door close with a soft thud below her, and she watched from her window as Gabe meandered back down the sidewalk until he faded into the darkness.

Then, Natalie lowered herself onto the bed with a sigh, her fingers toying mindlessly with the Christmas-themed comforter. It had been a strange evening. Strange, and sad, and... happy, too. Even exhilarating at times. She didn't know what to make of it, or of anything, really, because this town had cast some sort of spell on her, making her confuse left with right and up with down. Making her question her convictions, her hopes and dreams, her fears and heartbreaks.

It was probably for the best that she was leaving soon, she decided. But against all odds, she would miss the town—and the people in it—for many months to come.

Natalie didn't remember rising from the bed, or walking to her suitcase, or unzipping it and pushing her fingers past the folded jeans and T-shirts and the extra bottle of shampoo. But the red velvet box was in her hand all the same, and her heart had lodged itself at the base of her throat as she gently, reverently, carried it to the small table and chair set by the window.

She sank into one of the chairs, the box sitting loosely in her lap, and gazed outside for a long time, her eyes tracing the moon as it cast shimmering shadows on the snow-tipped trees. After a while, she lifted the box and set it on the table, staring at it as the minutes ticked past. Even though this box contained her most precious possession, she hadn't opened it in nearly twenty years.

She couldn't. The pain... it was indescribable.

But tonight? Well, maybe she was feeling a little braver tonight. Maybe she was simply missing the two people she loved the most, even now, even after all these years.

Or maybe it was because of the look in Gabe's eyes... the hope in them. Maybe she needed a reminder of why she couldn't stay in this town, why the memories it evoked would eventually drive her mad.

A quick flick of the wrist, and the box was open. Nestled inside was a delicate glass ornament—an angel holding a sign that said *Hallelujah*. Nothing special—on the outside, at least. Nothing noteworthy. Just a regular ornament, the kind that hung on hundreds, maybe thousands, of Christmas trees all over the country. Mass-produced.

That last Christmas, Natalie hadn't even liked the ornament all that much. She preferred the flashier things... or she used to, anyway—Santa Clauses riding in gift-stuffed sleighs, ice-skating penguins, a church with real working lights that could be turned on with the push of a tiny button. But tonight, as she turned that angel over in her hands, as she stroked its glass wings and traced the *Hallelujah* with her fingertips, she bowed her head and wept.

For everything that had happened, and for everything that could never be.

When she was finished, she tucked the angel back in the box, wiping the tears from the glass with the hem of her sweater. Then, knowing it deserved better than the bottom of her suitcase, she carried it over to the nightstand and slipped it in the very back of the drawer, out of sight.

But never out of mind. No matter how much she tried.

CHAPTER 10

"You're the prettiest elf I've ever seen," a little boy said to her shyly as she handed him his treat bag following his visit with Santa. This was said in a whisper so that his mother, standing nearby, didn't overhear.

Natalie grinned at him as she crouched to eye level. "I bet you say that to all of Santa's elves," she whispered back.

He considered her words for a moment, puckering his Cupid's-bow lips. Then, "Maybe," he relented. "Does that mean I'll get an extra gift on Christmas morning?"

Natalie laughed. "No, but it means you get an extra cookie right now." She led him over to the cookie table, giving Humphrey a wide berth on the way, and helped him choose a sugar cookie shaped like an ornament and decorated with red frosting and silver sprinkles. He took an enormous bite and grinned at her, his lips already stained red, and it was with no small measure of regret that she led him by the hand back to his mother.

Natalie had always wanted a little boy of her own. A girl, too, because wouldn't that have been perfect? Wouldn't that have been wonderful, if Devin hadn't gone and ruined things. If he hadn't destroyed, in one fell swoop, the carefully laid plans that she'd been building for so many years.

"Mommy, why is that elf so sad?"

Walter, hearing this, turned and raised his bushy eyebrows at her from beneath his Santa hat, and Natalie hurried to arrange her features into something less forlorn. *Don't scare the children, Natalie*, she scolded herself. *Don't scar them with the harsh realities of life.*

She plastered on a bright smile. "I'm not sad," she said to the girl who had spoken, adding a wiggle of her prosthetic ears for good measure. She rubbed her stomach. "I just ate too many Christmas cookies," she added with a wink. The girl laughed, and her mother grinned appreciatively, and Natalie was

Peppermint the elf again, performing her holiday duties with good cheer.

No one—and certainly not this young girl—needed to know that she'd spent the entirety of last night weeping into her pillow. No one needed to know that, even now, she was dying a little on the inside.

But children could sense these things, Natalie knew, because the next child in line, a boy who couldn't have been more than four, with chubby, angelic cheeks and ocean-blue eyes, shook his head when she offered him a treat bag. "You keep it," he announced with an adorable lisp. "Candy always makes me happy, and there's lots of it in there."

She could have kissed that sweet face, but she settled for a hug instead, reveling in the warmth and comfort of those little arms around her. When she pulled away, she passed the treat bag over the boy's head to his mother, who accepted it with a grateful smile, both women knowing he would probably regret his generosity the moment he stepped outside.

After that, Natalie did her best to perk up, though she didn't fail to notice the concerned looks Walter and Carol Miller were slipping her way at every available opportunity. Finally, mercifully, the last child plopped herself onto Santa's lap and began rattling off her list of Christmas wishes, ranging from a new pack of crayons to a unicorn she could ride to the moon. Walter listened with a twinkle in his eye and a faint smile on his lips, then deftly avoided promising her a unicorn before sending her on her way.

Natalie closed the door behind her, then turned to grab her coat, pretending not to notice Carol waving energetically from the cookie table, trying to get her attention. While she appreciated the concern, what Natalie needed most right now was to be alone, where she could unpack her thoughts... or pretend to, anyway, because in reality, Natalie was a master of avoidance. Self-preservation, she supposed, and really, could anyone blame her?

Peeling off her elf ears, Natalie headed toward the door, and was moments away from grabbing the handle when it was pushed open from the other side, letting in a frigid gust of winter air and one very cold-looking Gabe. "Hey," he said, his entire face lighting up when he saw her. Those butterflies in her stomach took flight again, but she did her best to push them back down, because they meant nothing. He meant nothing.

"I was hoping to catch you before you left." He

gestured toward Humphrey, who was staring at them in stoic silence while slowly munching on a carrot. "Have the two of you made up yet?"

Natalie scowled at the reindeer. "We have not. I'm fairly certain he's proud of what he did." There had been a certain... pizzazz... to his kick, but fortunately, Natalie's ribs were healing nicely, and the hoof-shaped bruise on her side was fading to a mottled yellow-green. She gave him another scowl, just for good measure, as Gabe chuckled.

"I hear he's quite cuddly, actually."

"Yeah?" Natalie cocked an eyebrow at him. "Then why don't you step into his pen and see if he wants a hug."

"Hard pass." Gabe was looking at her now with that intensity that had become familiar, but no less disconcerting. "As much as I'd love a little one-on-one time with Santa's best reindeer, I actually came here to see you."

"Oh?" What were those butterflies doing in there, dancing the tango? Natalie pressed a subtle hand against her stomach and feigned nonchalance, even though that almost-kiss from last night was burning a hole in her mind. "What can I do for you?"

His smile was slow and soft, yet somehow redhot, and Natalie crossed her arms over her chest to ward off the flame of desire that had suddenly ignited inside her. What was *wrong* with her? Okay, yes, he was a beautiful man, and apparently everyone in Chestnut Cove worshipped him, and he had been nothing but kind to her, a near-stranger, since the moment he found her abandoned on the side of the road, and...

Do you need any more reasons? a voice in the very back of her mind asked slyly. *Kiss him, you fool. KISS. HIM.*

"Are you okay?" Gabe was studying her face intently, his lips curved down in a frown. "You look a little... constipated." He grinned at her. "I can prescribe you something for that, you know."

"Gee, thanks." Natalie was torn between outright horror and the sudden, bizarre urge to laugh. She couldn't make up her mind, so what burst from her lips was a sort of strangled snort-laugh, a sound she imagined might come from a hog in the throes of labor. Gabe raised his eyebrows in amusement, but to his credit, he remained silent, watching her with a mildly curious expression.

Then, after another beat of silence, "Having a bad day?"

Natalie shook her head. "You have no idea." Having successfully rid herself of the elf ears, she slipped on her coat and buttoned it up to her neck in a vain attempt to conceal her costume. She'd quickly learned that a simple stroll down the sidewalk had children practically throwing themselves at her in ecstasy while rattling off their list of wishes they wanted her to pass along to Santa. Unfortunately, she'd once again forgotten a change of shoes, and as she and Gabe headed into the blustery air, she jingled with each step.

"Mind if I walk you back to The Mistletoe House?" Gabe asked. "I'm heading that way anyway —tonight is Holly's late night at the café, so I need to swing by and pick up Sophie." He grinned at her. "We're having a gingerbread house contest at my place. You're welcome to join us, if you'd like. Although I have to warn you, things can get a little competitive."

She hesitated. That all sounded wonderful—on the surface, at least. In reality, it would be a nightmare, conjuring up all sorts of memories for Natalie that were best left buried deep in the ground.

Gabe must have sensed her discomfort, because the smile immediately slipped from his lips, replaced with a look of chagrin. "Hey," he said, shaking his head, "no pressure, okay? I'm sure you're exhausted, and have had your fill of little kids for the day, and I probably shouldn't have asked."

"No, it's not that," Natalie started to say, but then stopped herself. She and Gabe might have struck up a friendship over the past few days, but they still knew very little about each other, and frankly, Natalie needed to keep it that way. For her own sake, as well as his, because soon, she was leaving, and whatever spark of attraction they had would be nothing but a memory.

"Actually, yes," she said, glancing sideways at him as they walked. Night was beginning to fall, the sky a gorgeous mauve highlighted with streaks of turquoise and gold, colors that could never be replicated on paper. "It's been a long day, and I'm just going to grab a bite to eat and call it a night. But thank you for the invite, and for thinking of me." She grinned at him, trying to lighten the mood. "Turns out playing Peppermint the elf is the hardest job I've ever had."

"I had a feeling it might be," Gabe said, "especially for a self-proclaimed hater of Christmas."

"I don't *hate* Christmas," Natalie said. "I just have an... issue with it, I guess you could say." She shrugged. "Not everyone loves all that festive stuff, you know."

Gabe chuckled. "I have literally never heard anyone say that before." Now it was his turn to shrug. "But to each their own, I suppose. At any rate, I knew you were probably ready for a day off, so I arranged for you to have one tomorrow."

"What?" Natalie stopped walking and stared at him. All around them, the trees in the town square twinkled softly with hundreds of strands of lights, casting a golden glow over his features. "Who's going to play Peppermint for the day?"

"Faith Holiday." Snow was beginning to fall around them, dusting the sidewalks in soft white. Gabe reached out a hand and lightly brushed away a snowflake that had landed on her nose, and under any other circumstances—in any other place, with any other man, in any other life—Natalie would have fallen in love with him on the spot.

"How did you manage to convince her to do that?" Natalie had a hard time squeezing the words past the lump in her throat. Gabe withdrew his hand, though his eyes continued lingering on her face.

"Let's just say I owe her a favor or two around the inn." Gabe's dark eyes crinkled in the corners as his lips tipped up in a smile. "But before you go thinking

I've done this out of the goodness of my heart, I should warn you... I'm not *that* selfless."

"No?" Natalie asked, her voice gently teasing. "That's not what I heard at the tree-lighting ceremony last night. When I first met you, I had no idea I was in the company of a god among men."

Gabe inclined his head. "I try." Then, grinning, he added, "Don't you want to hear my ulterior motive?"

Natalie laughed. "Do I want to?" The snowflakes were collecting on his dark hair, glittering under the waning sunlight, and Natalie had to repress the urge to brush them away. She didn't want Gabe falling for her. Just like she couldn't let herself fall for him, because Chestnut Cove was not, and would never be, a place she could call home.

Gabe exhaled softly, as though steeling himself for something. Then, his eyes never leaving her face, he said, "I was hoping to take you out on a date. Not just a date, but a full-day extravaganza."

"An extravaganza?" Natalie's eyebrows shot into her hairline. "That sounds exciting. Or maybe terrifying. Honestly, I'm not sure how to feel." She was flirting with him, despite her best efforts, because something about this man was electrifying. And *that* was terrifying. And exciting. And she was *leaving*, she reminded herself. She was leaving, and good riddance to this town of eternal Christmas, because even though she'd been playing the part since she arrived, her heart couldn't take much more of this.

"So… what do you think?" Gabe asked, cocking his head. "Are you game?"

"Oh, I'm game," Natalie found herself saying—all rational thought seemed to have left the building. "I'm absolutely game."

CHAPTER 11

*N*atalie awoke the next morning to a soft rustling sound in the hallway. Throwing back the covers, she padded across the room and opened the door just in time to find Faith tiptoeing away, doing her best to avoid the creaky floorboards on her way to the stairs.

"Faith?" Natalie asked, frowning at her in confusion. "What are you doing?"

Faith winced. "Sorry to wake you, dear. I had a special delivery for you, and I wanted to bring it by your room before I headed out for the morning. I already told Holly I would need a boatload of coffee before I attempted to stuff myself into that elf costume." She winked at her, then continued tiptoeing toward the stairs, the little gold bells on her Christmas sweater jingling merrily.

Natalie smiled to herself—she was beginning to like those sweaters, she decided, even if she wouldn't be caught dead actually wearing one. Then she glanced down at her feet, and saw several packages in Santa Claus wrapping paper waiting for her. "What's all this?" she murmured to herself as she bent down and lifted them into her arms. After carrying them inside and laying them gently on the bed, she tore off the wrapping paper on the first package and threw back her head in laughter.

Inside was a Christmas sweater that would rival the gaudiest one in Faith's closet, bright green and threaded with red garland. Ball ornaments in shades of silver and gold hung from various spots of the garland, and the background of the sweater was dotted here and there with white puff-ball snowflakes. It was the most hideous thing Natalie had ever seen, and tears of laughter were streaming from her eyes as she picked up the accompanying note.

Dear Natalie,

The moment I saw this sweater, I knew it was perfect for you.

See you soon,
Gabe

"He's not actually expecting me to *wear* this, is he?" Natalie muttered to herself, flicking one of the ornaments only to discover that it jingled, because of course it did. Then she spotted the P.S. at the bottom of the note.

Santa personally told me you won't be getting any presents for Christmas this year if you don't wear it.

"Okay, *fine*," Natalie grumbled, though she couldn't help grinning as she slipped the sweater over her head and shoved her arms into the sleeves. It was bag-shaped and perfectly awful, but it was also sort of adorable, and who would have known? Maybe Faith had the right idea after all.

The wrapping paper on the second package was torn off in short order, and Natalie actually clapped her hands in delight when she discovered a wrapped plate of decadent-looking cinnamon rolls inside, perfectly warm and perfectly gooey. "Okay, *now* you're speaking my language," Natalie said to the folded note taped to the plate, as if Gabe could hear her. She plucked it off and unfolded it, a smile curving her lips as she scanned Gabe's handwriting.

Dear Natalie,

A full stomach is a must in preparation for our extravaganza—doctor's orders. This is my mother's recipe, and I had to promise to take Sophie to a princess tea party in exchange for Holly showing me how to make them. The tiny terror wants me to wear a purple dress and a tiara, and she won't take no for an answer.

Holly says you must be worth it, and I have to admit, I agree.

Gabe

Natalie blinked back tears as she read and reread Gabe's note, her heart in her throat. No man had ever said anything like that to her. Devin loved her, she knew that—or at least he *used* to love her—but Natalie couldn't say that he cherished her. That he adored her. But Gabe... well, she could tell that Gabe was a man capable of cherishing a woman. How he had remained single for so long was a mystery.

The third and last package was bulky, and Natalie eagerly ripped it open to reveal a thick down jacket in a beautiful shade of caramel, lined with luxurious faux fur in soft beige. It felt heavenly between her fingers, and more importantly, it felt *warm*. Something capable of withstanding the frigid mountain air, something that wouldn't make her feel like a human popsicle.

Gabe's last note was short and sweet:

Dear Natalie,

You're going to need this today. I hope it fits.

Gabe

Natalie traced her fingers along his words, trying to imagine him sitting down to write these letters for her, to plan this day, to put so much thought into the things she might enjoy.

Suddenly, she couldn't wait to see him. She also had no idea what that meant… for either of them.

Her phone chimed then with a text, and she dropped the coat and hurried over to the nightstand to retrieve it, already rehearsing her thank-you message to Gabe for the thoughtful gifts. But when she swiped her finger across the screen, her pulse kicking up a notch with excitement, she didn't see Gabe's name…

She saw Devin's.

I miss you. Can we talk?

How could six words ruin a morning so quickly? A week ago—heck, even two days ago—Natalie would have been ecstatic to hear from him. Ever since she left, she'd known, she'd *known*, that he would realize he made a mistake. Checking her phone upwards of a hundred times a day had been draining and, frankly, humiliating, because she wasn't desperate. She wasn't, because she understood true desperation, and as much as she loved Devin, this was not it.

Still, though, she was lonely. Incredibly lonely… but lately, well, things were changing, weren't they?

Natalie stared down at the phone in her palm for several long moments, frozen with indecision, and then it chimed again.

Can I pick you up at ten?

Natalie's heart had seized up at the sight of Devin's message, but one glance at Gabe's name on the screen had some of the tension melting away.

Absolutely, she responded, deciding to thank him for his kindness in person. *Looking forward to it!* Then she set her phone back on the table and turned her attention to the plate of ooey-gooey cinnamon rolls. Lifting the cellophane wrapper, she caught a whiff of cinnamon goodness and moaned softly in anticipation. They were still warm, and she was famished.

Devin could wait. Maybe forever.

NATALIE WAS STANDING in front of The Mistletoe House at ten o'clock on the nose, eagerly scanning the town square for Gabe. The day was blustery but dry, though the mountains all around Chestnut Cove were glittering with newly fallen snow. It was a glorious sight, and Natalie inhaled deeply, her lungs reveling in the fresh mountain air mixed with the aroma of freshly baked cookies from The Chestnut Café next door.

In the distance, Natalie could make out a cluster of children waiting outside town hall for the doors to open for Santa's Wonderland, and to her surprise, a flicker of longing passed through her. In spite of the ridiculous costume, and the murderous reindeer, she was beginning to enjoy her time as an elf. Natalie laughed to herself as she imagined Faith in the role instead, though she had a feeling the older woman was born to be one of Santa's helpers.

Natalie craned her neck over a cluster of people passing by on the sidewalk, their arms weighed down with shopping bags, until she finally spotted Gabe's dark hair and broad shoulders bobbing above the crowd. She hurried to smooth down her hair, her heart jackhammering against her ribcage as he approached and their eyes met.

"Hi there," he said with a smile, looking genuinely happy to see her.

For once, Natalie didn't think; for once, she just acted, and a moment later, she was in his arms, her head nestled against his bulky coat as she breathed in his earthy scent of musk and pine. He seemed momentarily surprised, his body tensing for a brief second before he relaxed into the hug, his arms slipping around her waist, his chin resting in her hair.

"What was that for?" he asked when they pulled apart, earning a few teasing catcalls from a group of local men ambling by. Natalie's face heated, but she kept her gaze fixed on Gabe as he reached out a hand and tenderly stroked the pad of his thumb down her cheek. "Hello to you, too," he murmured.

"Hi." Natalie grinned up at him. "I had a very good morning."

"Did you now?" Gabe's smile was mischievous. "I can't imagine why." He nodded toward her down coat, a perfect fit. "New coat?"

"That's not all." Natalie unzipped the coat with a flourish to reveal the ugly Christmas sweater underneath. She wiggled her hips until the ornaments jingled. "What do you think?"

"I think I've never seen anything quite this beautiful." His gaze was on the sweater only briefly before it roamed over her face. "I had a feeling it would suit you. And it's the perfect outfit for our extravaganza. Our *Christmas* extravaganza." He had tucked her arm in his as they began walking down the sidewalk, shoulders touching, but his last words had Natalie stopping in her tracks.

"A… Christmas extravaganza?"

"That's right," Gabe said merrily, unaware of the color draining from her face. "I've seen you in action a few times as Peppermint the elf, and I've decided you don't hate Christmas as much as you think you do. So today, I'm on a mission." He spread his arms wide, his face lit with a grin. "A mission to bring back your holiday spirit. A whole day dedicated to Christmas, so you can remember how awesome it is."

"Is that…? Wow," Natalie managed, unable to form a coherent thought. She did her best to rearrange her features into what she hoped was an appreciative look, because Gabe… well, he looked incredibly excited, and proud, and he had *no* idea the treacherous, shark-infested waters he was treading in right now with no lifeboat in sight. "A Christmas extravaganza, huh?"

"That's right." Gabe slipped his hand into hers, giving her fingers a gentle squeeze. "I guarantee we're going to have a good time." His eyes met hers, dark and warm and filled with promise. "So, what do you say? Are you in?"

She was *not* "in." She was very much not "in," but

Gabe's eyes were searching hers, and those godfor-saken butterflies were tangoing in her stomach again, and Devin's message was playing in the back of her mind... and so she found herself saying yes.

But only she could tell she didn't really mean it.

CHAPTER 12

The sun was slipping toward the horizon and the sky was growing heavy with the promise of snow as Natalie and Gabe meandered through town later that day, hand in hand, clutching to-go cups of delicious hot chocolate and talking about their hopes and dreams.

"I always wanted kids of my own," Gabe said, his voice wistful as they passed the town hall. Santa's Wonderland was just closing for the evening, and Natalie did her best to sneak a peek of Faith in her elf costume to no avail. A little boy and girl, presumably brother and sister, were arguing good-naturedly over who got the biggest cookie from Carol, while nearby, a toddler had plopped himself in a snowdrift and was refusing to leave without seeing Santa one more time. Natalie's heart ached as she looked at him—the rosebud lips, the chubby cheeks, the wide, angelic eyes.

"Me too," she murmured, glancing at Gabe to find him gazing at the toddler too, his eyes filled with the same longing she felt. "Two, maybe three. Four if I thought I could handle it." She laughed softly. "When I was a little girl, I used to dream of having a big family."

"Only child?" Gabe asked, raising his hot chocolate to his lips and taking a long sip. Natalie nodded, but offered no further comment. "Growing up, I used to wish I was an only child," he said with a laugh, nodding toward The Chestnut Café. Holly was visible through the window, wearing her flour-dusted apron and chatting with a pair of customers examining the bakery case. "Holly's a few years younger than me, but we fought all the time, driving our mother up the wall. Only when we got older, and our parents passed away, did we start to grow closer. Now, I don't know what I'd do without her and Sophie."

Natalie was curious about Sophie's father, but she didn't know Gabe well enough to broach the subject. Instead, she merely said, "You're lucky you have each other."

"We are," Gabe replied, then fell silent for a time. The streetlamps were winking on all over town, casting the sidewalk in a halo of light. Above their heads, the first stars were twinkling in a dusky sky that seemed to stretch to infinity, broken only by the distant mountain peaks. This place was beautiful, Natalie thought, a true paradise, a treasure practically hidden from the outside world. Despite her fears, today had been wonderful in every way. She slid a glance Gabe's way only to find him watching her carefully.

"What?" she asked with a nervous laugh. "Do I have chocolate on my mouth?"

"No." Gabe still looked uncharacteristically serious, and something shifted in the pit of Natalie's stomach. "I was... wondering if I could ask you something. A personal question."

Why don't you like Christmas?

Natalie was steeling herself to blurt out whatever canned response she could come up with in a split second, but Gabe surprised her by asking instead, "What happened with your fiancé?"

"Oh." A relieved breath escaped Natalie. "*That.*" She considered his question for a moment, frowning slightly. The day she met Gabe, she'd told him that her fiancé had just broken up with her, but he hadn't asked any questions, and she hadn't offered any information. Now, though, she was ready to talk about it.

"I'm not sure, exactly," she began slowly, trying to gather her thoughts. "Devin and I were together for seven years, and I thought we were happy. When he told me that we were over, I was shocked, and heartbroken, and completely devastated, really."

Gabe nodded. "I'm sure," he murmured, giving her hand a light squeeze. "Breakups are tough, especially if they're out of the blue."

The two of them had come to a pretty wrought-iron bench, and Gabe used one gloved hand to wipe the snow away before they took a seat. In the spring and summer months, this bench would overlook a lovely garden that had been planted in the middle of the town square, but right now, its branches were bare, its ground frozen—a different kind of beauty, Natalie decided. An unexpected kind.

"But that's the thing," Natalie said as they settled onto the bench, close enough that their legs were touching. "Was it really out of the blue, if I take a step back and look at things objectively? He had been spending more time at work and with his friends, and less time with me. We didn't talk as much as we used to; we didn't laugh as much. The romance was pretty much dead in the water, although I guess I figured that was normal. I mean, sparks don't last forever, do they?"

She paused and met Gabe's eyes. "We had become roommates, and it happened so slowly that I didn't even realize it. And I don't think he did, either. Devin isn't a bad guy... I just think he wanted something more. Something better. And while I wish he had gone about things differently, I'm starting to wonder if we were really meant to be. If we were really soulmates, like I'd always assumed."

She bowed her head, studying the last wisps of whipped cream floating on her hot chocolate. "He was my first real relationship, and I think I clung to him because I finally wasn't alone anymore." She shrugged. "That's what I've decided, anyway. Maybe Devin has an entirely different story to tell." Another pause, longer this time. "He contacted me today."

Gabe's entire body went still. Then, softly, "What did he say?"

Natalie swallowed hard, blinking back tears. "That he missed me. That he wants to talk." She toed at the cobblestone beneath her feet. "I didn't answer him yet. I don't know if I ever will." She let out a bitter laugh. "At least that's what the logical part of me says—'don't answer, he doesn't deserve to hear from you.' But…" She trailed off with another shrug.

"But seven years is a long time to share your life with someone," Gabe finished off with a sigh. "And part of you wants to know if you can make it work."

Natalie rubbed her temples with her gloved fingertips, trying to ward off the first signs of what promised to be a raging headache. "Yes? No? Truthfully, I don't know. It all happened so fast, and the wound is still new." She lifted her cup to her lips and drained the last of the hot chocolate, warmth flooding through her and settling in her stomach. Then she gave him a chagrined look. "I feel like I shouldn't be discussing this with you. We're supposed to be on a date here."

Gabe's expression was mild. "Isn't that what dates are for? To get to know someone?" His lips tipped up in a smile. "Besides, I'm the one who asked."

"True." Natalie returned his smile with a crooked one of her own. Then, with a nudge to his side, she said, "What about you? I spilled my guts all over this bench, so now it's your turn. Have you had any significant relationships?" She already knew the answer, thanks to Faith, but Natalie was dying to learn more. The more she got to know Gabe, the more she couldn't believe that some woman had let him slip away.

"One." The smile fell from Gabe's face as his eyebrows drew inward. Natalie was watching him intently; now it was his turn to stare into his cup, swirling the contents as he considered what to say next. "Her name was Maria. We met on our first day of medical school—we happened to pick seats next to each other during orientation. We dated all throughout school, rotations, residencies... I really believed she was 'the one.'"

"What happened?" Natalie asked, unable to stop herself.

Gabe's face darkened; it was the first time Natalie had seen him upset. "What happened is that my father got sick. My mother had been battling cancer for years and was too weak to care for him. Sophie was just a toddler, and Holly already had more than she could handle between being a single parent and trying to run the café. So I made the decision to move back to Chestnut Cove. I hadn't planned on returning... as you can see, there aren't many job opportunities here," he added with a flick of his hand around the town square. "But Doctor Mills was nearing retirement age, and I offered to buy him out of his practice. The rest is history."

Natalie waited for him to continue. When he didn't, she prodded, "And Maria? I take it she didn't come with you."

"She did not." Gabe's gloved hands tightened almost imperceptibly around his cup. "She told me she wasn't cut out for small-town life, that she wanted no part of Chestnut Cove, and gave me an ultimatum: my family, or her." His smile turned wry. "Obviously you know which one I picked."

"Wow." Natalie rested her hand on his forearm. "That's… brutal."

Gabe nodded. "It was. But it also gave me a lot more insight into her character—turns out, I didn't know Maria as well as I thought."

They were both silent for a time after that, watching the people strolling past them. Several smiled and waved, a few gave them curious looks. Natalie mulled over everything Gabe had told her, trying to find the parallels in their stories. Her fingers grazed her pocket, searching for her phone; she'd switched it to silent before their date, and part of her was dying to know if Devin had reached out again. "Did she ever try to contact you?" she asked, turning back to Gabe. "After things were over, did she ever reach out?"

"Once." Gabe shifted closer to her on the bench,

and on impulse, she rested her head on his shoulder. "She called my practice here in town and left a message. I never called her back." He shrugged, and Natalie's head rose along with the movement. "What would be the point? There was nothing left to say, for either of us."

Natalie gazed up at him—his strong jaw, his windswept dark hair, those kind eyes that currently held a hint of hurt. "Did you ever regret that?" she murmured, her mind back on Devin, on what she would—and should—do.

Gabe merely shook his head. "No, because she had already shown her true colors. Even if she wanted to apologize, or reconcile, or whatever she had in mind... it was too late, because to me, she would never be the same woman I fell in love with. Our relationship would always be tainted by what she had done—abandoning me when I needed her the most." He swallowed hard, Adam's apple bobbing. "My parents died within three months of each other. I could have used her support, but she thought living in a place with nightlife was more important than me."

"I'm sorry," Natalie said. "For both of us." She laughed softly. "Relationships suck."

"Sometimes." Gabe's fingers gently stroked the

ends of her hair. "But sometimes they can be wonderful, too. Opening up your heart to another person is never easy, but I'd like to think that it can be worth it." He fell silent after that, and she spent the next several minutes listening to the steady, reassuring beat of his heart. Somewhere in the distance, a child's laughter cut through the quiet, and the soft melody of Christmas music lifted up from the town's ever-present carolers. To her surprise, Natalie found herself humming along.

"So did you have fun today?" Gabe asked, breaking the silence between them. His hands were still in her hair, and her head was still on his chest, and she thought, briefly, that she might be able to stay like this forever.

"I had an amazing time," she said, and meant it. "It was truly unforgettable."

Despite the terror that had squeezed her heart like a vise when Gabe first told her their plans, the day had been magical from start to finish. Their first stop had been to an old-timey theater on the edge of town, where they watched a marathon of classic Christmas movies over tins of hot buttered popcorn and giant sodas. Natalie had been entranced by each of them, and by the time the credits rolled on *It's A*

Wonderful Life, tears were streaming down her cheeks.

They'd left the theater hand in hand, then headed to their next stop: an outdoor ice skating rink that circled a beautifully decorated Christmas tree. Natalie could barely walk in the skates Gabe had helped her lace up, and her first order of business upon stepping onto the ice was to fall flat on her face. When she'd finally managed to remain upright for more than two seconds, Gabe had patiently led her around the rink, her arm tucked firmly into his, as she slipped and slid and shrieked with glee, his own laughter mingling with hers in the wintery air.

"You're the most beautiful couple," an elderly woman had said to them as they sat on the bench outside the rink a little while later, unlacing their skates. "I can tell how much you're in love." She pressed her hand to her chest, right above her heart. "You remind me of what my husband and I were like when we were young. Merry Christmas to you both."

Neither of them had bothered to correct her, because the woman's eyes were filled with tears as she walked away. They'd merely looked at each other shyly before Gabe broke the awkward moment by announcing their next stop: a cookie-decorating class at a local bakery. The theme was Christmas—of course—and for the next hour, she and Gabe had a blast designing sugar cookies in the shapes of Santa Clauses, reindeer, candy canes, trees, stockings, and gingerbread men. They had even more of a blast eating them, Gabe teasing her when she took an enormous bite of a tree only to come away with a frosting-smeared mouth, Natalie responding by wiping a fingerful of red frosting on his chin.

Dinner had followed at a nearby restaurant, where their conversation had been easy and natural, and now they were here, on this bench, neither of them willing to end the night.

With this on her mind, Natalie murmured, "Thank you, again. You didn't need to go through all this trouble... although I have to say, this is the best date I've ever had. By about a million lightyears."

Gabe chuckled, warm and soft, filling her soul with golden light. "I absolutely did. So tell me." His arm tightened around her. "What do you think of Christmas now?"

"Let's put it this way," Natalie said with a smile, pushing aside the pain his innocent question elicited. "I dislike it a little bit less than I did this morning." She held her thumb and forefinger a millimeter apart. "Like this much, although that might be generous."

Gabe threw back his head and laughed. "I'll take it."

Then · he lowered his head and their gazes snagged, and in the space of several heartbeats, a hundred unspoken words lingered in the air between them, visceral, electric. Natalie's heart was in her throat, and her pulse had kicked into a frenzy, and his eyes were locked on her lips as she shifted closer to him on the bench. The world around them faded away, the hustle and bustle of people passing by them became a blur—in that moment, only they existed.

Their lips were nearly touching, his hands were in her hair, the rest of Chestnut Cove was entirely forgotten... and then Natalie's phone rang, shattering the silence into a thousand pieces. Red-faced, breathing erratically, she scrambled for her purse, and why exactly was she answering the phone again? Oh, right, because Gabe was trying to kiss her, because she *wanted* him to kiss her—desperately— and because they shouldn't.

"Hey, Natalie, it's Vernon," a gruff voice said when Natalie greeted the caller on the unfamiliar number. "I just wanted you to know that I was able to pull a few strings, as promised, and the parts we needed for your car arrived this morning. I'm putting the finishing touches on everything tonight, so you can pick it up first thing tomorrow morning. Then you can be on your way."

"Oh." The word came out on a soft sigh, and the breathless anticipation of only a few moments ago had morphed into a dull, painful thudding in the pit of her stomach. It was time to go. It was time to leave Chestnut Cove, and Gabe… forever.

The moments ticked by in silence, Gabe's curious gaze on Natalie's face, Natalie's own gaze on the zipper of her coat, because she simply couldn't look at him right now.

"You there?" Vernon sounded puzzled. "I thought this would be good news."

"Oh, yes… it is," Natalie stammered. "It is good news, and thank you, Vernon. Thank you very much. I'll see you tomorrow morning." She hung up the phone and stared down at the dark screen, her mind blank. This was how it was *supposed* to go, she reminded herself. Chestnut Cove was a temporary stop—a very temporary stop, because it wasn't her final destination. It couldn't be, because she didn't belong here.

But oh, how she wished she did. In another time,

in another life... how she desperately wished she did.

Gabe was still silent, watchful, and the electricity in the air had evaporated, because he had heard. He had understood. She chanced a glance at him, and noticed that his face was carefully blank. "I take it your car is ready?" he asked softly, so softly his words were nearly swept away into the night.

Natalie nodded. She didn't trust herself to speak. She thought of her foster family, how it would feel to turn up on their doorstep, how Jennifer and Todd Sanderson would do their best to welcome her, to make her believe she was family.

She wasn't, though. She never would be, and that wasn't their fault. She understood that, but it didn't erase the sadness, or the emptiness, or the void.

"Is there any way you can stay?"

She was positive she'd heard those words, but when she looked up at Gabe, he was gazing into the distance, his eyes on the mountain peaks, the twinkling stars overhead, the inky darkness that stretched in all directions.

She didn't answer him. Not just because she wasn't sure he'd really spoken, but because she had no idea what to say.

CHAPTER 13

The next morning, Natalie's heart was heavy as she drove her car away from Vernon's shop, back toward The Mistletoe House. Faith had been asleep by the time Gabe had dropped Natalie off at the inn; Natalie had tapped lightly on her door but received no response, and her room was dark other than the soft glow of the Christmas tree lights spilling out into the hallway. Natalie had left, disappointed, and spent the next hour packing her suitcase so she could leave right after breakfast.

She wasn't sure why she had wanted to see Faith so badly. Maybe she wanted to return her elf costume so the older woman could find a replacement as soon as possible, and keep the town's biggest Christmas event running smoothly. Maybe she wanted to share one last mug of hot cocoa with her by the inn's fireplace, which had become something of an evening ritual for the two of them once Santa's Wonderland was closed for the day.

Maybe she just needed someone to talk to.

Gabe had been quiet and solemn as the two of them had walked back to the inn, his hands shoved deep in his pockets, her heart thumping dully at the base of her throat. They'd said goodbye on the threshold, neither one of them quite meeting the other's eye.

"Is this it?" he had asked, his voice uncharacteristically gruff.

"What? No!" Natalie had replied, stricken by the thought. She thought she caught a flicker of hope in his eyes—there and gone in an instant—and she'd quickly said, "I'll stop by your office before I leave to say goodbye."

The light in his eyes had dimmed at that, and when he walked away, his head bowed low against the cold, Natalie had tears in her eyes. He had gotten to her. He had reached into some deep, broken part of her, and together, the two of them had created something that had the potential to be special. That had the potential to be beautiful. That had the potential to last a lifetime, and beyond.

She knew it. She could feel it.

And here she was, walking away.

The view out of Natalie's windshield was blurry as she wiped away a fresh wave of tears, averting her eyes from the holiday shoppers crowding the town's quaint cobblestone streets. She had to circle around the block twice before she found a parking space near The Mistletoe House, and when she slid out from behind the wheel, she was surprised to find Faith standing in the inn's doorway. The older woman's arms were crossed over her chest as she watched Natalie cross the street, her eyes sliding back and forth between Natalie and her car.

"Don't tell me you're leaving already!" she said the moment Natalie was in earshot. Her tone wasn't accusatory... exactly... and Natalie found herself shifting uncomfortably from foot to foot under the woman's stern gaze. Faith scowled at Natalie's car. "How is that done already? Vernon is usually slower than a snail running a marathon, but somehow he managed to get your car back before Christmas?"

"He called in a favor for me," Natalie replied. "He knew I was anxious to leave."

Well, she *had* been anxious to leave. Now... not so much.

"I'll need to have a word with him," she could

have sworn she heard Faith mutter. Then, more loudly, "What are we going to do without an elf?"

"Right." Natalie straightened her shoulders, even though she felt about two inches tall. Faith *had* realized this was a temporary gig... right? Somehow it didn't feel that way, and Natalie couldn't figure out why. "Well, I figured that Jeannie would probably be over the flu by now, and—"

"She's not," Faith cut in. "I just spoke to her last night. She sounds terrible. She could barely get her words out, she was hacking so hard." She shook her head. "The children would get sick for Christmas, and they'd be *so* disappointed."

Natalie stared at Faith, her heart sinking as a sense of déjà vu washed over her. Now that she'd met the kids, now that she'd seen the awe on their faces, the glow of excitement, the wonder...

"I... I guess I could manage another day or two," she relented, and something inside of her shifted, as if a weight had been lifted from her soul. "Just until Jeannie is better."

"Just until Jeannie is better," Faith replied, clapping her hands once, a combination of enthusiasm and finality. "Wonderful, Natalie, I knew you wouldn't abandon us in our hour of need."

That sounded just a *tad* overwrought, Natalie

thought as she swept past Faith on the way to her room, but she couldn't keep the grin off her face all the same.

"NATALIE! There you are. Just the woman we wanted to see."

Carol Miller slid into the seat across from Natalie, gingerbread latte in one hand, Holly's signature sugar cookie in the other, and motioned to Walter, who was standing by the pastry case at The Chestnut Café, his belly touching the glass as he debated his options while Holly stood patiently by.

"Walter, over here!" Carol called, gesturing animatedly to her husband. He held up a finger, indicating that she should wait, then turned his attention back to Holly before pointing to an enormous slab of cherry cheesecake.

"That man can't see a dessert without sampling it for himself," Carol said with a good-natured shake of her head as she watched Holly slide the cheesecake onto a plate and pass it across the counter to Walter, whose eyes lit up with glee. He paid for the treat, then strolled over to the table where Natalie was sitting—and now Carol, and apparently Walter too.

MIA KENT

The three of them had just finished their shift at Santa's Wonderland, and after removing her elf costume and jingle shoes, Natalie had hightailed it to the café to send out another round of resumes in her never-ending job hunt. So far, she hadn't had a single bite, and even though she wanted to chalk up the silence to the approaching holidays, Natalie feared she would soon be out of options... and worse, out of money.

Despite her fears, Natalie closed her laptop and smiled at the older couple before taking a sip of her espresso hot chocolate, another Holly specialty—both delicious and completely necessary after a little girl had thrown up all over Santa's chair, necessitating a one-hour cleanup that largely fell on Natalie's shoulders.

"That was some day today, wasn't it?" she asked, watching Walter shoveling cheesecake into his mouth with reckless abandon. He paused only to nod, while Carol watched him with an expression somewhere between horror and love.

"Eh, we've seen worse," he said with a wave of his hand. "Do this for another thirty years, and you'll have plenty of stories of your own."

"I'm sure I would," Natalie said, resting her hands on her laptop, her mind rotating through the list of jobs she'd applied for over the past couple of days. A few of them seemed promising, sure, but none of them felt *right*. Not like the ice cream shop had, the first time she'd stepped inside and that cool, sweet air had hit her lungs. Of course, Devin had been there too... which reminded Natalie that she'd never returned his message. The ease with which it had slipped her mind surprised even Natalie.

Lost in thought, she hadn't realized that Carol was studying her until she glanced up to find the other woman's eyes locked on Natalie's face. "So what did you want to talk about?" Natalie asked, her fingers itching to return to the keyboard. The days were ticking by, the money in her bank account was dwindling to alarming numbers, and as much as she would have liked to sit and chat, she simply didn't have the time.

After exchanging a look with Walter, Carol gestured toward Natalie's laptop. "I know you've got a lot on your mind, so I'll cut right to the chase. Walter and I have a job available on our farm, and if you want the position, it's yours."

Natalie reared back in surprise as a grin formed on her lips. She was a city dweller, and had been for all of her life. The idea of her tramping around on a farm in muddy boots and overalls... well, it was ridiculous. Completely ridiculous.

"I appreciate the offer," she said with a laugh. "Truly, I do. But I think you may have gotten the wrong impression of me—I've never even visited a farm in my life, let alone worked on one." She shook her head. "I don't know a thing about them."

Nor do I want to. She kept that last thought to herself, because the offer was lovely, and Carol and Walter were even lovelier. Her nose wrinkled at the thought of goats, and pigs, and... manure. So much manure.

Carol laughed. "It's not what you think. While we do have a few animals puttering around, our focus is mainly fruits and vegetables, and seasonal offerings —berries and peaches in the summer months, corn and pumpkins in the fall, Christmas trees in winter. We have hayrides, corn mazes, and scarecrow-making contests in the fall, horse-drawn carriage rides and hot cider in the winters, and just about everything in between. We sell our produce to local markets and restaurants, and then we have our own farm store where we offer homegrown canned goods, jams and jellies, apple and pumpkin butter, fresh cider..."

Carol spread her hands wide. "As you can imagine, we're pretty busy, and as we get older, Walter and I are starting to slow down a little."

"Speak for yourself," Walter said, licking a smear of cheesecake from his lips. He laughed richly and patted his belly. "I'm just as strong and limber now as I was when I was a young buck."

Carol gave him a wry look. "Well now you're an old buck, and I don't think I imagined all the moaning and groaning I heard yesterday when you were unloading crates in the back of the store." She turned her attention back to Natalie. "We only have one child—our son, Leo—and he chose not to follow in our footsteps on the farm. He's a botanist working in research at a university a few hours from here, and while we couldn't be prouder of all that he's accomplished, we need help. Desperately. We want someone to manage our farm store, and then eventually expand into other things, like events." She cocked her head curiously at Natalie. "Didn't you say you managed an ice cream shop before you ended up here?"

"I did," Natalie said, "and I loved it. The job on your farm, well... it sounds fantastic." And it did, truly, a dream job, and one she would have jumped on in an instant if it were anywhere else. *Anywhere* else but this town of eternal Christmas. So it was with no small measure of regret, and sadness, that she shook her head. "But as wonderful as it sounds, I'm afraid I'm only going to be in town a couple more days. As soon as Jeannie is back on her feet, I'm headed out."

"I see. Well, I sure am sorry to hear that." Carol took a sip of her gingerbread latte, though her eyes never left Natalie's face. "And where will you go after here?"

Natalie hesitated. "I don't know," she admitted after a few moments. Carol and Walter had never asked about her background, and she'd never volunteered any information. "I haven't quite figured out my next steps yet, but I've been applying to jobs around the area, and I'm sure something will turn up soon."

Carol was silent for a few beats. Then, "I see," she said in a mild tone. "Well, like I said, Walter and I think you'd be the perfect fit..." She gestured to Walter, who nodded emphatically, his snow-white beard bobbing up and down. "And we'd hate for you to say no without even seeing what we have to offer. Tell you what." She tapped the table with her latte cup, once, with finality. "Our farm is a little off the beaten path, and you might have trouble finding it on your own. Why don't you ask Gabe to bring you by, and we'll give you the full tour. *Then* you can say no."

Natalie froze at the mention of Gabe. She had no idea where they stood. Yesterday had been wonderful, and magical, and their almost-kiss had stolen her breath away—she hadn't been able to stop thinking about it. But the tone had shifted completely after Vernon called, and their walk back to The Mistletoe House had been awkward, to say the least. She promised she would stop by his office and say goodbye before she left, and she intended to keep that promise. Otherwise...

Carol leaned forward, her eyes impossibly soft, impossibly kind. "Honey, can I ask you a question." When Natalie nodded, she said, "Are you sure you want to leave Chestnut Cove? We have a wonderful community, you know, and it seems like you've been enjoying yourself here." She trailed her fingers over the rim of her cup, eyebrows furrowed as if she was debating what to say next. She glanced at Walter, who nodded and pushed aside his empty plate.

"Gabe is a good man, you know," he said, his eyes steady on hers, a grandfatherly expression on his face. "As steady as they come. We've known him since he was a boy, and he seems to be quite taken with you. In fact," he added with a chuckle, "ever since you showed up here in town, that boy has had a grin on his face and a new spring in his step. He's a good man," he repeated.

"I'm sure he is," Natalie said after a beat, swallowing hard, her heart folding in half. "But my home isn't here. It's…" *Nowhere.* "Not here," she finished, looking everywhere but into Walter's kind eyes.

Carol nodded. "Okay," she said, reaching across the table to rest her hand gently on Natalie's wrist. "You don't owe us any explanations, honey, and we aren't going to pry. But if you change your mind, just know we'd love to have you."

Natalie nodded, her eyes on the table. "Thank you," she murmured. "That means a lot."

The conversation drifted to different topics after that, but Natalie had a hard time concentrating. While she normally enjoyed being in the Millers' presence—in some ways, they reminded her of her parents, or who her parents could have been—today, she was anxious for them to leave.

Fifteen minutes later, they did, with Walter waving goodbye to everyone in the café and Carol tugging him out the door before he could order a second slice of cheesecake to go. Natalie watched them leave, then sighed and opened her laptop once more, ready to resume the job search. She was just logging into her email when Holly passed by the table with a cart, stopping to collect Natalie's empty cup and plate.

"Another round?" she asked, brushing back a few strands of hair that had escaped her ponytail. She was wearing her usual frosting-stained apron, and today had accessorized it with dangling Santa Claus earrings.

"No thanks." Natalie patted her stomach. "If I keep this up much longer, I'll have to go shopping for new clothes." Then she eyed the tray of cookies in Holly's cart. "But do I really care?" she asked, snatching an enormous chocolate chip one.

Holly laughed. "I understand the dilemma, believe me." She nodded toward the door. "I saw you talking with Carol and Walter. They're wonderful people, aren't they?"

"They are," Natalie agreed around a mouthful of cookie. She raised her napkin to her lips to brush off the remaining crumbs. "They've really taken me under their wing since I've been here—they even offered me a job at their farm store. I guess their son Leo doesn't live around here..." She trailed off as she noticed Holly's entire body language shift. At the mention of Leo's name, the smile had slipped from her lips, and tension began emanating from her in waves.

Natalie peered at her closely. "Is everything all right?"

Holly gave a little start, then shook her head. "Everything's fine!" she said with an emphatic wave of her hand. Then she grinned at Natalie. "Just trying to remember if I added sugar to my latest batch of red velvet cupcakes. Would you believe I once grabbed the salt instead of the sugar and added a whole cup to the mixing bowl? You should have seen my customers' faces when they bit into it, but of course, this is Chestnut Cove, so everyone was too nice to complain." She laughed, though Natalie noticed that it didn't quite reach her eyes.

"Anyway," she said, tapping Natalie's table, "I'll let you get back to work. If you want anything else, you know where to find me."

"Thank you," Natalie said, her eyes drifting back to her computer screen. "I might—" Then she stopped short with a gasp. "Oh my goodness. Oh, *yes*! Finally! Finally finally *finally*!" She was doing a wiggle dance in her seat while Holly watched in amusement.

"Good news?" she asked, nodding to the screen.

Natalie nodded, her gaze still locked on the intro

line of the email that had come in just five minutes ago. "A job interview for a manager position at a bakery." She pressed her hands to her cheeks, shaking her head, still unable to believe her eyes. "It was my first choice, too!" She leaned back in her chair with a sigh of relief. "Now *that* is good news."

Holly laid a hand on Natalie's shoulder. "That *is* good news, Natalie. I'm happy for you."

"Me too," Natalie said. "Me too."

And even though she meant it, for the rest of the day there was a heaviness in her soul, one she was entirely unable to shake.

CHAPTER 14

atalie awoke the next day to a mountain of snow outside her window and the sound of Vernon's snow plow scraping the streets. Otherwise, traffic on the roads was nearly nonexistent, and the normally bustling sidewalks were empty. Faith had informed her by text message that Santa's Wonderland would be closed for the day due to the inclement weather, and so Natalie spent a wonderful morning in a cozy chair by the window, alternating between watching the snowflakes drift gently to the ground and losing herself in one of the books Faith kept stocked in the library downstairs.

She was going to miss this place. She was going to miss it terribly, but it was time to move on. The interview was scheduled for next week, a few days before Christmas; the bakery was eager to find a replacement for their current manager, who was planning to stay home to raise a new baby, and Natalie was equally eager to hear more about the job. By all accounts, it seemed like the perfect fit.

Except...

Well. Except.

Shaking off that last thought, Natalie picked up her book again, though a few minutes passed before she realized she hadn't read a single word. Vernon had done a good job of clearing the streets, and the citizens of Chestnut Cove were venturing outside again, picking their way around snowdrifts—or, in the case of two little boys in puffy coats and thick scarves, launching into an energetic snowball fight that had passersby laughing and ducking. Someone had flipped on the twinkle lights strung around town, and the animated Santa Claus on the corner was waving and ho-ho-hoing to everyone who passed.

Natalie didn't see Gabe at first—not the flash of dark hair, or the broad shoulders that rose above the other pedestrians. His head was bent against the cold, his nose buried in the plaid scarf he wore so well. Natalie's eyes were glued to him as he rounded the corner and approached The Mistletoe House, and when she saw him turn and continue up the inn's sidewalk, she bounded out of her room, flew down the staircase, and yanked open the front door just as he held up his hand to knock.

"Hi." He looked at her in surprise, one hand still poised in front of the door.

She smiled at him, her heart lighter than it had been all day. "Hi. I saw you coming." It occurred to her then that he may not have been coming for *her*, and her cheeks flared pink.

Then he gave her a soft smile, and her embarrassment melted away. "Can I come in?"

She laughed. "It isn't my house, so I can hardly say no." She stepped aside as he brushed past her, bringing with him the earthy scent of pine and clean, fresh snow. He stood in the foyer, uncharacteristically awkward, his dark eyes on her face as she gave him an uncertain look.

She had just opened her mouth to say something —though she hadn't the faintest idea what—when he beat her to the punch. "I heard about the job." His tone was mild, neutral, as if he were merely reporting the weather, or something equally mundane. "Congratulations." He tipped his head in acknowledgement, and her heart, which had been jackhammering mere moments ago, plummeted into her stomach.

"Thanks." She crossed her arms over her chest, suddenly cold. "It's just an interview, though. I don't want to get ahead of myself."

He nodded, his eyes solemn. "I'm sure you'll get it. Why wouldn't you?"

She probably would—or at the very least, she had an excellent chance. All the right qualifications, and her introductory telephone conversation with the owner of the bakery had gone very well, their personalities immediately compatible. She could have told him all of that, but instead, she changed the subject, nodding toward the frosted window. "Terrible out there today."

"Really?" Gabe asked mildly. "I think it's beautiful." He brushed some of the snow from his shoulders, showering the floor around them. "I was supposed to host a clinic today for those who don't have medical insurance, but so many people called to cancel that I ended up having to reschedule. I have the entire day off." He was gazing into her eyes now, and the butterflies that had become a constant presence once again took flight.

Natalie nodded, unable to look away. "It must be nice to have some time to yourself."

"Not really." Gabe's gaze intensified, and she shivered. "I spend too much time by myself. I was hoping for a little company today."

"Oh?" Natalie's throat was dry; she could scarcely get the word out. "Are you planning to take Sophie somewhere?"

"No." The accompanying head shake was slow, meaningful. "I had such a wonderful time the other day, I thought maybe you might be up for another outing."

She choked out a laugh. "Another Christmas extravaganza?"

He shrugged. "Whatever you want it to be. I'd really love to see you, though."

"Gabe." Tears sprang to Natalie's eyes, entirely unexpected. "I'm leaving, you know."

"I know." He held out his hand, and she slipped her fingers into his, the gesture intimate, automatic. "But you aren't leaving today."

"No," Natalie said softly. "I'm not."

"I'm glad to hear it." Gabe smiled, his eyes crinkling in the corners, and... *was* she falling in love with him? There was a lightness about her, a golden glow, a feeling of rightness with everything in the world whenever he was around. And yet, she couldn't picture them together. They were from different worlds, and there was no place for her in his.

But oh, how she wished there could be, if only for a little while.

"Shall we?" Gabe's smile deepened as he tucked his arm around her. After she grabbed her coat and shoes, he led her to the inn's front door, holding it open so she could slip outside into the snow squall that had suddenly kicked up. She drew her face against his chest, laughing, her nose aching, her eyes stinging from the cold.

From the *cold*, she repeated to herself. And not because of him.

FIFTEEN MINUTES LATER, after a semi-harrowing drive deeper into the mountains, Gabe's pickup truck bounced over a final snowdrift before he pulled into the dirt lot in front of an adorable red farmhouse. A snow-covered tractor was parked beside them, and a flurry of clucks and squawks rose up from a henhouse nearby, though its occupants didn't venture outside to greet their visitors. Acres of fields lay all around them, mostly barren except for one section that held rows of small pine trees and a sign that said *Choose Your Own Christmas Tree!* A couple of people were tramping through the snow, heavily bundled up against the cold as they perused the trees.

Beside the farmhouse was a barn surrounded by a wooden fence, and though Natalie could hear the muffled moos and bleats of farm animals, they remained tucked inside. Beyond that was another farmhouse, smaller and more weathered-looking, with a beautiful wraparound porch that was decorated for Christmas, and a wooden sign above the front door with *Miller Farm Market* etched in fading white letters.

"Here we are," Gabe said, cutting the engine. He smiled as he gazed out over the snowy farmland. "I've been coming to this place since I was a kid. My mom and Carol were good friends, and we used to stop by every Sunday after church to see what fruits and vegetables were in season. Sometimes Carol would have freshly made fudge for sale —it was her secret recipe, and the taste was indescribable. My sister and I lived for that fudge when we were kids."

"It's a beautiful place," Natalie said, glancing around, taking in the acres and acres of land, the farm equipment, the mountains that rose behind it.

"A lot bigger than I pictured." She frowned at Gabe. "Walter and Carol run this place by themselves?"

"They have seasonal workers who help with the planting, harvesting... and whatever else needs to happen on a farm." His grin was sheepish. "My knowledge on that topic is next to nothing. We came to Miller Farm to buy and eat, not to grow. But the bulk of the work they do themselves." He shot her a curious look. "Why the interest? I was surprised you wanted to come here, of all places. I didn't take you for an outdoorsy person."

Natalie shrugged. "To tell you the truth, I'm not sure what I am. I get the sense I'm still figuring that out. As for why I wanted to come here?" She hesitated. "Well, Walter and Carol happened to mention it in passing, and I thought it would be fun to see the farm for myself." She didn't mention the job offer to Gabe, nor was she entirely sure why she wanted to visit Miller Farm in the first place. When the two of them had left The Mistletoe House, Gabe asked what she might like to do, and this was the first thing that came to mind.

Gabe spread his arms wide. "Well, here it is. Shall we go inside? Now I've got fudge on the brain, and it might just be my lucky day." He slid out from behind the wheel, then rounded the truck to help Natalie navigate the slick lot. Someone—presumably Walter —had shoveled the parking area and thrown down some salt, but a few patches of ice remained. Natalie clung to Gabe's arm as they headed for the shop, and a blast of warmth hit them as they stepped inside.

"Welcome to M—oh! Hello there." Carol waved merrily at them from behind the counter. "What a wonderful surprise! I was just telling Walter that I hoped we'd have some visitors today. Most folks don't want to venture out in weather like this, and it makes for a long day. You know me, I like the company."

"And *I* like the fudge," Gabe said, rubbing his hands together gleefully as he spied the display case filled with at least ten different varieties of home-made fudge. He made a beeline for it while Natalie began perusing the shelves stocked with delicate glass jars of jams, jellies, and preserves, each wrapped with a Christmas-themed bow and arranged by variety. She was debating whether she wanted to try apricot or blackberry preserves—or maybe both, and a raspberry one too—when Carol sidled up to her with a smile.

"Are you reconsidering our offer?" she asked in a voice that carried across the room.

Natalie winced and glanced over at Gabe, whose

attention was concentrated so fully on Carol's fudge that she was positive he hadn't heard a thing. Then she shook her head. "No," she said softly, ignoring the twist of guilt in her stomach. Guilt, and something else too... something that felt a lot like regret. "I'm sorry."

"Me too." Carol patted her arm. "We would have had a lot of fun." There was no annoyance in her tone, but the second twist of guilt was sharper than the first. "Now if you'll excuse me, I'd better see what that man of yours is doing," she added, pointing toward the counter.

Natalie opened her mouth to correct the older woman—Gabe wasn't *her* man, as lovely as that would have been—but Carol was gone before she could fully form the sentence. Instead, she watched the two of them for a while, Gabe pointing eagerly to the fudge, Carol laughing as she cut him an enormous slab, both sharing some inside joke that Natalie had no part of.

But deep down, she knew that she *did* want to be part of it. Desperately.

Her eyes lingered on them for a few more seconds, then she wandered over to a gently boiling pot of hot apple cider that sat alongside paper cups and a selection of sugar cookies Natalie immediately recognized from The Chestnut Café. As Gabe and Carol continued to talk, she ladled a generous portion of the cider into a cup, then savored its warmth between her hands before raising it to her lips and taking a long, leisurely sip. The flavor was wonderful—cinnamon and orange peel, brown sugar, a hint of cloves? Natalie couldn't be sure, but a second sip soon followed, then a third, and before long, the cup had been emptied and refilled two more times.

"You ready to head out?" Gabe's breath was warm on her ear as she turned to find him standing beside her, holding three containers filled to the brim with fudge.

"You've got quite the appetite," she said with a smile, nodding toward the containers.

"I wish," he replied with a look of regret. He held up the first container. "This one is for me." Then the second. "This is for some of my homebound patients —they haven't tasted Carol's fudge in a while, and I know they miss it." The third container, he gently placed in her hands. "And this one is for you. To remember us by."

Natalie stared down at the fudge, tears filling her eyes, feeling ridiculous because this was *fudge*, for crying out loud. "I don't know what to say," she whispered. She dimly registered Carol watching the two of them from behind the counter as she raised a shaky hand to wipe her eyes. "You're a wonderful man, Gabe. Thank you."

He gave her a gentle, teasing prod to the side with his elbow. "It's just fudge," he said softly. With the pad of one thumb, he blotted the lone tear trailing down her cheek, and at his touch, her eyes drifted closed as she lost herself in the moment. Then reality slammed back into her—*hard*—and her eyes flew open again. He was watching her, his gaze tracing her face, and Carol was now motionless behind the counter, as if she feared even the slightest movement would disturb this moment.

"It's not just fudge," she said, wiping the remaining tears away with a rough swipe of her coat sleeve. "It's… it's *everything*. From the moment we met, you've treated me with such kindness. You've welcomed me into your community, and made me feel like one of your own. You made me feel like I had a family, and…" She hesitated, a lump forming at the base of her throat as she glanced away. "Well, that's something I haven't felt in a long time."

Carol was tiptoeing backward through a swinging door behind the counter, leaving just the two of them. Gabe's gaze was intense, penetrating, as if he were looking into her soul. "Stay," he murmured, raising his hand once more, his fingers brushing her cheek, tracing the lines of her jaw. "Please. Let's see what this could become."

"I can't." Natalie glanced away again, the lump in her throat now a balloon threatening to cut off all air supply. "Chestnut Cove is a beautiful place, but for me, it's different. It reminds me of a time in my life... a difficult time... that I've spent so long trying to overcome. That I've spent so long trying to forget."

"Talk to me." Gabe took a step closer, electrifying the air around them with his presence. "Let me help you. Let me understand."

"No," she said sharply, automatically. "I don't talk about it. Ever." The last word was spoken in a whisper, but the finality of it rang throughout the room louder than any gong.

Gabe was silent for several long moments, then he nodded, his eyes never leaving her face. There was sadness in them, and understanding too, and it was all Natalie could do not to break down completely. He reached out, his fingers brushing the ends of her hair, his eyes roaming over her face as if he was trying to memorize everything about her.

"If you can't stay," he murmured, "then let's enjoy whatever time we have left."

CHAPTER 15

Several hours later, Natalie was still wiping away tears—although this time, they were tears of laughter as she and Gabe examined her handiwork.

"It looks... nice?" he said in a hesitant voice. Then, seeing her brows furrow, he immediately amended, "It looks beautiful. Stunning, in fact. The most professional-looking wreath I've ever seen."

"It looks like it's been through the ringer," Natalie said, dissolving into another round of laughter as she held up the raggedy wreath she'd spent the past hour meticulously crafting. She and Gabe were back in downtown Chestnut Cove, participating in a wreath-decorating contest hosted by one of the local churches. Despite the weather, half the town seemed to have shown up, with people of all ages crowding around the long tables set up in the church's multi-purpose room to show off their design skills.

Natalie's wreath was the most pathetic-looking of the bunch, with a crooked plaid bow on top, a snowman that looked half dead dangling from the bottom, and an assortment of ribbons, tiny ornaments, glitter, and feathers haphazardly glued around the sides. Natalie had chosen the feathers on a whim, hoping to achieve a funky, festive look; instead, the wreath looked like it had been on the losing end of a fight with a barn owl.

Natalie eyed Gabe's own creation with a scowl. "How did you get it to look so perfect?" Indeed, his wreath, complete with perfectly symmetrical bows, glittery faux snow, and sprigs of holly, looked like it had walked right off the pages of a holiday maga-zine, while hers closely resembled something that had spent the past five years in the dump.

Gabe raised one shoulder in a playful shrug. "What can I say? I'm a man of many talents." Then he picked up her wreath and examined it with a critical eye, a smile playing across his lips. "I don't know what you're so mad about. I think it's adorable. Just a little tweak here..." He tried and failed to reattach the snowman, but its head only dangled further off the bottom before it slipped off altogether, crumpling to a sad heap at their feet. "Whoopsie," he said with a grin.

"Stop trying to sabotage me," Natalie said, yanking the wreath from his hands. She poured another generous helping of glue onto the frame, then picked up the snowman and shoved him back into place. Then, carefully, she carried her wreath to the table and presented it to the judges—Faith, along with two older gentlemen Natalie hadn't yet met.

"It's… well, it's interesting, isn't it?" one of the men said, adjusting his glasses as he leaned in further to study the wreath. He ran his weathered hands over one of the feathers. "Definitely unique."

"That's the ugliest thing I've ever seen," Faith hooted, slapping her hand against her thigh as she doubled over with laughter. She glanced at the two men beside her, then pointed to the slumping snowman. "Should we create a new award? 'Most likely to scare the children?'"

"Very funny," Natalie said, pinching Gabe in the arm and eliciting an *owwww* after she heard his snort of laughter. She turned the wreath around, admiring it once more. "You know what? I'd like to respectfully withdraw from the competition. This little beauty is coming home with me."

"I always did believe in Christmas miracles," Faith said with a wink. Then she handed her a participation certificate—Natalie had noticed several preschoolers proudly displaying their own— and Natalie and Gabe left the warmth of the church hall and stepped back into the frosty winter air. Their conversation quieted as they navigated the snowy sidewalks, Natalie's arm tucked in Gabe's once more.

When they reached his truck, which was coated in another fresh layer of snow, he helped her into the passenger seat, then leaned in toward her. "If you're up for it, I have one last thing in mind before we call it a night."

Natalie, who was in no rush to head back to the inn, readily agreed. The soft notes of "O Come, All Ye Faithful" were floating out from the radio as Gabe drove through the quiet streets, and Natalie hummed along to the familiar melody as she gazed out the window at the dusky purple sky, highlighted in brushstrokes of coral and teal where the sun was slipping beneath the mountains.

A short time later, they pulled into the driveway of a beautiful yet humble cabin tucked back into a grove of towering pine trees whose boughs were bent under the weight of the snow. Soft twinkle lights were strung around the front porch, and a family of softly glowing mechanical snowmen were waving to passersby. An evergreen wreath with a red bow hung from the front door, and the windows were framed with garland.

"I haven't had time to finish decorating the outside yet," Gabe said as he slipped his key into the lock on the front door and turned the knob. Natalie's eyebrows shot up as she glanced around at the outdoor decorations—of which there were plenty—but she kept her observations to herself.

Until Gabe pushed open the front door and the two of them stepped inside.

"Oh, my…" Natalie breathed, covering her mouth with one hand as she tried to comprehend what she was seeing. Somewhere inside the house was, well, an actual *house*, with furniture and walls and a television and all the normal things one might expect, but Natalie couldn't see any of it, because it looked as if a Christmas decoration warehouse had exploded over every surface.

She had no idea this many Santa Claus figurines existed in the world, let alone in a single cabin in the middle of nowhere. Santa Clauses on motorcycles, Santa Clauses with fishing poles. Santa Clauses gobbling cookies, Santa Clauses drinking ale. Santa

Clauses petting reindeer, Santa Clauses wrestling with penguins. Santa Clauses here, Santa Clauses there, Santa Clauses every-freaking-where.

"Uh," Natalie said, because her mind was otherwise blank. She gave Gabe a questioning look.

He grinned. "My mother started the collection when she was a kid, and I continued it. Now I have hers, too... between the two of us, I think we've amassed upwards of three hundred of them." He traced his finger down the motorcycle-riding Santa's back wheel. "Every Christmas, my dad would carry boxes and boxes of these little guys down from the attic, and my mother always waited until I was around so we could set them up together. We used to get such a kick out of them. Someday, I hope to pass the tradition along to my own children."

If Natalie wasn't so horrified, she would have found them funny—maybe even adorable—but her feet seemed to be frozen to the floor. She glanced around her, taking in the dozens—no, *hundreds*—of Christmas touches all around Gabe's house, from the standard wreaths and candles to more unique decorations, like a chipped porcelain Santa kneeling beside an infant in a manger, his hat in his hand.

"Ah, yes, the praying Santa." Gabe tenderly lifted it from its spot on the mantel and held it out for her to admire. "This was my mother's ultimate favorite, and mine too. It reminds me that Christmas is about so much more than decorations, and presents, and hot chocolate. It's about something more. Something much more."

As he returned the figurine to its place of honor, Natalie wandered around the cozy cabin—trailing her fingers along a snowman throw blanket, examining an antique tabletop sleigh pulled by plastic reindeer, coming face to face with a human-sized wooden elf holding a velvet bag of wrapped gifts. The entire time, her heart was in her throat, her stomach was vaguely nauseous, and her eyes were filled with tears she was careful not to let Gabe see.

Because she would have loved this. She *used* to love this. Christmas had been her favorite time of the year, the most magical part of her childhood, until that magic had been permanently banished from her heart.

"I know this seems like a bit much—in fact, I *may* have gone a little overboard with the decorations this year, but..." Gabe shrugged. "Why not go all out, right? So many of these decorations I inherited from my parents when they died, and they have such a special meaning for me, and for Holly too. She and Sophie live in an apartment and don't have too much space for decorations, so they love coming here and seeing everything... you should see how my niece's eyes light up whenever I bring out the Santa Claus collection. My mother..."

He trailed off and cleared his throat, and when he spoke next, his voice was low, rough. "She would have loved to have been here for that, so this is one small way I can honor her, keep her spirit alive for the granddaughter who barely remembers her."

He stopped speaking then, and Natalie was silent too, each of them lost in their own thoughts, their own memories and heartbreaks. "It's lovely," Natalie finally said, after an almighty internal struggle to banish her thoughts—lock them up and throw away the key, just so she could function. "And your home is beautiful."

For the first time, she noticed the Christmas tree by the front window, lost amid the rest of the decorations, undecorated except for a few strands of lights that remained unplugged. "Did you run out of time?" she asked with a small smile, pointing toward the tree. "I can't imagine how long all this decorating must take you."

"Too long," he admitted with a laugh. Then he stepped toward the tree, brushing his hands against its bare branches, which emitted the faint scent of pine. "But no, I didn't run out of time. I always save this for last, and for a special day, too. Usually Sophie and Holly come over and help me hang the ornaments—we go all out, with music and hot chocolate and more cookies than our stomachs can handle. But I thought that this year…" He hesitated, looking almost shy. "Well, I thought that this year, you and I might do it together. Give me something to remember you by, once you're gone."

Oh… oh, no. No no *no*. Not this, anything but this, but Gabe's face was earnest, and he had done so much for her—*so* much, and, well… it also sounded kind of wonderful, didn't it? The two of them, huddled around the softly glowing tree as the snow fell from the darkening sky and Bing's voice floated out from the old record player in the corner. It sounded kind of magical, the way things should have been.

The way things could still be?

Gabe took a step closer to her, his dark eyes roaming over her face, all traces of shyness gone from his expression. "Would that be okay?" One corner of his lips curved up in a smile. "You know, seeing as you don't like Christmas and all."

Natalie wasn't sure how it happened, or who made the first move, but suddenly she was in Gabe's arms, and his hands were in her hair, and around her waist, and their lips were touching in a kiss that was new yet somehow familiar, like an old song that was nearly forgotten until someone played it again. The kiss... oh, the kiss. It was warm and gentle, and soft... so soft, his lips on hers, exploring, leisurely at first and then with an urgency that nearly broke her. Then it was fire and passion, and her soul was singing with happiness, and rightness, and the knowledge that this moment, right here, had been written in the stars for an eternity.

When Gabe finally pulled away—it could have been seconds, it could have been years, but it most definitely wasn't enough—he stared at her, his chest rising and falling in time with her own. "Wow," he whispered, raking his hands through his dark hair, looking at her in disbelief, and awe, and something that looked a whole lot like love. "Just... wow."

Natalie couldn't have agreed more.

CHAPTER 16

*O*ver the next couple of hours, as she and Gabe slow-danced to the Christmas music crackling out from the old record player, her head on his chest, his arms encircling her waist, the moon full and the snow swirling outside the window, and then made a batch of his mother's famous hot cocoa, laughing like teenagers when she spilled the first sip all over her sweater... Natalie was having the time of her life.

On the outside, at least.

The inside was a very different story. The battle raging within her was intense, a true war between her head and her heart, the past she couldn't escape and the future she wanted so desperately. It was right in front of her, there for the taking, reach out and she could grasp it in her hands and hold on for dear life.

She could make this place her home. She could embrace the Christmases of her childhood, the *before*, the time when the world was bright and shining and full of love instead of darkness and grief and an unbearable, unyielding, unshakeable sadness. She could live in this town, and be welcomed by this community, this *family*, and she could be happy.

Finally, she could be happy. She could move on.

But every time she opened her mouth to tell Gabe that maybe, possibly, she could stay, something stopped her. Sometimes it was a memory, once-happy but now sharp and painful, pulling her down beneath the surface as she gasped and struggled and begged for air. Sometimes it was a flashback to the day, the hour, the moment it all went terribly, horribly, permanently wrong.

"I think we're almost finished here." Gabe stepped back from the tree they had been decorating and cocked his head, assessing their handiwork. Like the Christmas tree of Natalie's childhood, Gabe's was a jumble of ornaments and lights, beautiful in its chaos, mismatched yet perfect all the same. It didn't belong in a department store, or in the pages of a magazine.

It belonged in a home.

"Time for the star?" Natalie asked, approaching Gabe's side, slipping an arm around his waist and resting her head on his shoulder. There had been many stolen kisses over the course of the evening, each more thrilling than the next, each causing the warring portions of Natalie's mind to pick up their arms and head into battle once more.

"Not yet." Gabe held up a finger. "I always save my mother's favorite ornament for last." He bent down and began rummaging through the massive plastic container that held his ornaments and lights. "Ah! Here it is." He lifted out a small cardboard box, plain, clearly not the ornament's original home. "To tell you the truth, I never understood why this was her favorite," he said to Natalie as he pried open the box with his fingertips and slid off the lid. "It's a little plain for my taste, but maybe you'll disagree..."

He held up the ornament, which rotated slowly on its string. A delicate glass ornament—an angel holding a sign that said *Hallelujah*. Nothing special, like he said. Nothing noteworthy. Just a regular ornament, the kind that hung on hundreds, maybe thousands, of Christmas trees all over the country. Mass-produced.

Natalie took one look at it and doubled over in pain, and heartbreak, and a deep, bottomless grief.

Then, ignoring the sound of Gabe calling after her, she was running—out the door and into the frigid winter night.

CHAPTER 17

*S*anta's Wonderland was eerily silent at this time of night as Natalie sat in the shimmering silver sleigh alongside countless wrapped presents waiting to be delivered on Christmas Eve. She hadn't expected to find the town hall unlocked, nor was she surprised when she turned the handle on the front door and it yielded to her instantly—that was the kind of town Chestnut Cove was. A place where people trusted each other, and supported each other, and welcomed everyone, strangers included.

Natalie included.

Wiping her wet eyes with a shaky hand, Natalie glanced around, her eyes lingering on the velvet rope that separated Santa's throne from the line of children who would be here tomorrow, waiting for their chance to see him. Despite her initial reluctance, and her initial fear, Natalie had loved everything about her role as Santa's helper. She'd loved feeling like part of a family, for the first time in so long. She'd loved bearing witness to the pure, unadulterated joy on those children's faces, the wonder that filled their eyes, the anticipation, the belief that Christmas truly was the most wonderful time of the year.

She loved so much about this town, and the people in it—and one person in particular—but she understood now that she couldn't stay, because it had never been an option. Not really. Just a trick of the imagination, a sleight of hand, a misguided belief that she could be anything other than who she really was.

She didn't belong here. She knew it the moment she arrived, and she knew it now.

But that didn't make the prospect of leaving any less agonizing.

The minutes ticked by in silence as Natalie leaned her head against the sleigh seat, the tears spilling from her eyes, slowly at first and then streaming down her cheeks in twin rivers that stained her jeans and splattered onto the festive wrapping paper surrounding her. Those tears soon became sobs, the full-body kind, the kind that had her doubled over and gasping for breath, and oh, the *pain* of it all, the regret for what might have been, and—

"Natalie?" There was a creak as the front door closed, and then Gabe was walking toward her, his eyes shadowed with concern. He approached the sleigh. "I thought I might find you here." Nodding toward the piles of gifts surrounding her, he asked, "Is there room for one more?"

Natalie hesitated, then shifted a few packages until Gabe was able to squeeze in beside her, his knee and shoulder pressed against hers, the scent of him filling every inch of that sleigh and causing a fresh wave of tears to build behind her eyes. He was silent for a moment, then reached out and took her hand, a simple gesture filled with so much tenderness, so much kindness, that Natalie crumpled.

He stroked her hair as she wept for all she had lost, then and now, and all that she would still lose, including the moment when she left this beautiful town in her rearview mirror, forever.

When she finally quieted, he used the pads of both thumbs to wipe away her tears, his touch lingering on her face, before he looked her in the eyes and murmured, "Please, Natalie. Please tell me."

She took a deep breath, preparing once more to say no, but then... something inside her shattered. Face still streaked with tears, she gazed out the window, where the snow-dusted trees were just visible through the inky darkness. Then, softly, "My parents died on Christmas Eve. When I was eight." She heard Gabe's sharp intake of breath as the memories of that day flooded over her, but this time, she didn't fight them. She didn't battle against the unrelenting current. She just let them come.

"We'd spent the day decorating the whole house, inside and out—for whatever reason, we did the bulk of our decorating the day before Christmas, I guess to make everything seem even more festive. My mother baked cookies with me, I helped hold the ladder while my father hung lights from the roof. And we always saved the Christmas tree for last." Natalie dabbed at her eyes with the sleeve of her sweater. "My parents liked to make an event of it— there would be appetizers, and hot apple cider, and my mother's favorite records on the stereo. I got to stay up late, and we ended the night by looking out the window, watching the skies to see if we could spot Santa's sleigh." She let out a shaky laugh. "My father swore up and down that he saw him flying above the clouds, but I'm pretty sure it was just an airplane."

As she was speaking, Gabe had his arm around her, but she barely registered his touch.

"At the end of the night, we all went upstairs to get ready for bed, and my father asked me to turn off the Christmas tree. He'd forgotten to unplug it, and we never left it on overnight. Ever." The memories of her bounding back down the stairs were crystal clear... and then everything went blank.

"I don't know what happened... Maybe I looked out the window again, trying to find Santa's sleigh. Maybe I went to the kitchen to grab another cookie —which my mother told me *not* to do, since I'd already had so many. Whatever it was, I got distracted, and I forgot to turn the tree off. That night..." She stopped speaking and swallowed hard, and after that, her voice was barely a whisper.

"The investigator never could say for sure exactly what happened, but he suspects one of the wires was frayed on the strands of lights my father used. Whatever the reason, the Christmas tree caught fire in the middle of the night. We were sleeping... a neighbor happened to be awake, and he was able to grab a ladder and prop it against my window. He tried going back for my parents, but by then..." Her tone was dull now, wooden, robotic. "The fire... I remember how hot it was. And strangely, how beautiful it was, too. Powerful, almost magnetic. I was looking at the house, watching it burn to the ground, watching my parents die... and I was hypnotized."

She scrubbed at her cheeks with her hands, trying to claw away the memories. Then she looked at Gabe, her eyes hollow. "It was my fault. If I had just unplugged the tree like my father asked, I would still have parents." She stared down at her hands. "Needless to say, I don't celebrate Christmas anymore."

There was a long pause, an eternal pause, and then Gabe started to speak. Natalie interrupted him with a shake of her head. "Please don't tell me it wasn't my fault, that I was only a kid. I've been told that my entire life. Not a single person who's said that to me has ever walked in my shoes."

Another pause, then, softly, "I wasn't going to say that. I was going to say that I'm sorry, Natalie. I'm sorry for everything you lost, and I'm especially sorry that I tried pushing all of my Christmas cheer onto you. If I had known..." He laughed softly, though the sound held no mirth. "Suffice it to say that I'm horrified with myself. You told me you didn't like Christmas, and I should have accepted that without question." He looked up, and directly into her eyes. "Please forgive me."

Natalie waved away his words. "It's not your fault. You couldn't have known, and I could have told you to stop at any point." She shook her head. "The truth is, I think that part of me was enjoying the whole 'Christmas is amazing and magical' thing. I used to love the holidays more than anything, and you helped me to remember that. You helped me to escape from reality for a little while." She smiled softly. "Tonight, for the first time, being with you... I actually thought I could move on. I thought I could be happy, and normal, and the person I was always meant to be. I *was* happy, Gabe. You made me happy, you gave me joy, and that's something I haven't felt in a long time. Not truly."

He nodded slowly, considering her words. Then, after another long moment of silence, "I'm glad. But the ornament...?"

He left the rest of the sentence unfinished, and Natalie's heart cracked as she pictured that unremarkable glass angel. "We had the same one when I was a kid. In fact, it was the last Christmas ornament my mother ever bought. Months after the fire, when the house was being demolished, one of the workers found it in the ruins. Everything around it was destroyed by the flames, but somehow that little angel was left untouched."

Her breath hitched as she recalled her grandmother presenting it to her—"a miracle," she'd called it. Natalie had carried it with her from that day on; the angel was the one constant in her life, especially after her grandmother died and she entered the foster care system. Natalie told all of this to Gabe, then finished with, "And when I saw you holding that same ornament tonight, something in me just… cracked." She stared down at her hands again. "It's my own fault. It was stupid of me to think that I could be anything other than what I am."

Gabe took her hand in his, and when she finally met his gaze, his eyes were haunted. "You're leaving, aren't you." It wasn't a question, because he already knew the answer.

Mutely, she nodded.

"Is there anything I can do to change your mind?" He swallowed hard. "Please don't go, Natalie. Please… don't go."

"I have to," she said, her voice trembling. She raised her hand to gesture all around them. "You have a beautiful life here, Gabe. You have a beautiful town, and wonderful neighbors, and you've been…"

She shook her head, pressing her lips together, unable to continue for a moment. "You've been like something out of a dream. Like something out of someone else's life." She lowered her voice to a whisper. "I'm leaving, Gabe, because I have to. This life… it just isn't the one for me."

CHAPTER 18

"We're so looking forward to having you work here, Natalie. See you on Monday?"

"I can't wait," Natalie said, rising to take the hand of the owner of the bakery where she'd just interviewed for the position of manager. The two of them had spoken on the phone twice prior to today's meeting, which ended up being a formality—the job was Natalie's, if she wanted it.

Which she did. Sort of.

"And Natalie?" the owner said as Natalie made her way to the door. When she turned, the other woman offered her a warm smile. "Merry Christmas."

"Merry Christmas." Natalie tried not to sound as half-hearted as she felt, and as she headed out the door, she averted her eyes from the gingerbread house display in the bakery's front window. Not that it mattered, of course, because as soon as she stepped outside, she found herself in the middle of a crowd watching a Christmas Eve parade pass by, Santa bringing up the rear, perched in a firetruck and waving to the kids screaming in excitement. An elf hurling bags of candy managed to knock her right in the nose, and she winced and tried to rub away the pain before slipping through the crowd, head bowed against the chilly air.

Only one more day, she reminded herself. A little more than twenty-four hours from now, she wouldn't have to think about Christmas again for an entire year.

Her cell phone chimed with a text message, and she slid it out of her pocket.

I'm here. Grabbed us a table by the window. Can't wait to see you. XX

Natalie stared down at the message for several seconds, her heart in her throat. Then, with a sigh of resignation, she checked the directions she'd written on a square of paper prior to the interview. To his credit, Devin had agreed to meet her at a coffee shop only a few blocks from the bakery, which was more than two hours from his home. The drive certainly wouldn't have been an easy one, especially on Christmas Eve, and with the forecasters warning of a white Christmas. Fortunately, Natalie didn't have to worry about the weather—for the time being, she was staying in a hotel room in the city, with plans to find a more permanent place to live after the new year.

As she strode through the city streets, nose burning from the cold, she couldn't help but notice how the passersby just... well, passed her by. They were staring at the ground, or else their noses were buried in their phones, and not a single person greeted her, or even glanced her way as they hurried about their business. Not like in Chestnut Cove, where Natalie couldn't walk more than a few feet before running into someone she knew—or someone she was *about* to know, because strangers very quickly became friends.

She missed it. More than she thought she would, like a constant ache in the pit of her stomach. And she missed Gabe. She missed him terribly, and—

No, she reminded herself firmly. *Do not go there.*

Gabe was in the past—a brief but beautiful memory, something to hold on to in the darkest hours of the night, and nothing more.

Natalie's stomach dropped to somewhere in the vicinity of her feet as she approached the coffee shop and saw her ex-fiancé through the window, his head bent over his phone, a mug of coffee in front of him. He looked so comfortable, so at ease, while Natalie's heart was slamming so hard against her ribcage she feared that something might break. Her mind wandered unconsciously to Humphrey the reindeer, and an unexpected wave of longing washed over her. Despite their tenuous relationship, she even missed glaring at him from across the room when none of the children were looking, and okay, yes, she might have slipped him a cookie or two, or two dozen, because he *was* pretty cute. In a beastly sort of way.

A rush of warm, fragrant air greeted her as she shouldered open the door to the coffee shop, but instead of heading to the counter to order, she walked directly to Devin's table, yanked out the chair across from him, and sat down.

He glanced up, startled, and then his eyes softened as they roamed over her face hungrily. "Hi," he said, reaching across the table for her hands. She stared at his outstretched hands for a moment, then tucked hers firmly into her lap. He winced. "Okay, sure, I definitely deserve that." Letting out a long breath, he raked his fingers through his hair. "Thanks for meeting me," he said. "I was hoping we could... you know. Talk."

"So talk." Natalie could feel a tic going in her jaw as she looked at him, the man she had loved, and adored, and planned a life with before he burned it all to the ground. She had no intentions of making this easy on him, because he certainly hadn't given her that same consideration when he blew up her life without warning.

And ultimately, sent her into the arms of the man she was always meant to be with.

Her eyes burned with tears as she thought of Gabe, the agony scrawled across his face that last night together, when she told him she was leaving. More than a week had passed since she'd last seen him, or heard his voice, and the void he left in her heart—no, her *soul*—was bottomless.

"Oh, Natalie, I'm so sorry." This time Devin managed to successfully grab her hand. He looked pained as he reached across the table to brush away her tears. "I'm so, so sorry. I don't know what I was thinking, I must have been out of my mind..." He shook his head roughly. "I've gone through everything over and over in my head, and I guess—I don't know, I guess I got cold feet? The prospect of spending a lifetime together just made me freak out, and that's not your fault, it's mine. But it only took five minutes after you walked out that door for me to come to my senses, and ever since then, I've been missing you like crazy."

He paused, presumably waiting for her to say something. When she remained silent, he squeezed her hands tightly. "I want a do-over. I want to make things right." He brushed away the fresh wave of tears that had formed and were now trickling down her cheeks. His voice softened. "I don't ever want to make you cry again."

At this, she looked up, her expression hardening. "I'm not crying over you, Devin. And I haven't been crying over you for weeks." His face went slack, but her voice was steel. "I only agreed to meet with you today so I could tell you in person to stop calling me. Stop texting me. Stop believing for even a single second that I would consider taking you back. Seven years, Devin. Seven *years*, and you discarded me on the sidewalk like a piece of trash."

She stood from the table, tucking her purse over her shoulder, ignoring the curious stares of the other patrons. "I also wanted you to know something else.

While it's true that I loved you for the past seven years, it's only taken a few weeks for me to realize that I was never *in* love with you. And you were never in love with me, either, because if you were…" Gabe's face was in her mind again, and the words were stuck at the base of her throat. "If you were, you would have begged me to stay."

She took a step back from the table. "So goodbye, Devin, and… have a nice life. I mean that. Truly. Because at the end of the day, that's what each of us deserves."

And then, without further ado, she was gone, closing the door to the coffee shop—and closing that chapter of her life, forever.

THE CHRISTMAS EVE parade had largely dispersed by the time Natalie was headed back to her hotel, though many children and their parents had lingered downtown, exploring the shops that were still open, or exclaiming over the window displays— though they were a poor comparison to Chestnut Cove's, Natalie thought. After sidestepping a little boy belting out "I Want a Hippopotamus for Christmas" to anyone who would listen, and then giggling hysterically, Natalie rounded the corner and came face to face with a little girl of around eight huddled up on a bench with her parents, the three of them enjoying hot cocoa and candy canes.

Natalie winced; their perfect little family was a dagger to the heart, so reminiscent of her own before it all went so horribly wrong. Her parents had lived for Christmas—every year, it was a weeks-long event that started the day after Thanksgiving and continued well into the new year.

Once, when Natalie was six, she'd begged her father to leave up the Christmas tree, and he had obliged—by the time the Fourth of July had rolled around, they were decorating it with red, white, and blue bows, and by Halloween, her mother declared that a haunted Christmas tree would be the perfect addition to their spooky décor. She could so clearly remember the two of them making ghosts out of Styrofoam balls, white garbage bags, and twist ties, then hanging so many from the tree its boughs were bent almost to the ground.

What would her mother think of her now?

That last thought shot through Natalie like a bullet, her lungs constricting to the size of pinholes as countless Christmas memories unfurled in her mind like a ball of yarn coming undone. Old records on the stereo, Bing's voice filling every nook and cranny of the house. Sugar cookies baking in the oven, the air redolent with the scent of almond and vanilla, Natalie's lips stained green from the spoonfuls of icing she'd snuck whenever her mother turned her head. Her father humming carols to himself as he unwound countless strands of lights while Natalie sat at the old piano, plinking out notes, trying to match the song.

They'd poured so much time into the holidays, so much love... how would they feel, knowing that their only daughter could no longer bear to celebrate the day that meant so much to them as a family?

They'd be devastated, Natalie knew. Absolutely devastated.

Another memory then, this time of her grandmother, the old woman's wrinkled face wet with tears as she presented Natalie with the angel that had somehow survived the fire untouched. "It's a Christmas miracle," she'd whispered, her voice filled with wonder as she held Natalie tight. "A sign from your parents that they love you, and that they're all right."

Natalie had never believed that. For her, that angel was simply a fluke, something that had been in the right place at the right time. Nothing more, nothing less.

Her heart squeezed painfully as she pictured its face, so perfect, so peaceful, having survived an unimaginable tragedy. For thirty years, she'd carried it with her, a reminder of all that she had lost, a final connection to the parents she missed so desperately.

But... what if her grandmother had been right? What if that angel *was* one last message from her parents, reminding her that miracles did exist, even in the darkest of times... and that she should live her life to the fullest, with love and hope and joy, until they could meet again.

As she was lost in thought, and lost in memories, Natalie's feet had carried her to the hotel where she was temporarily staying. She hurried through the lobby, then jammed her finger repeatedly on the elevator button until the doors opened. Her mind was on her suitcase, on that little angel tucked safely inside... the angel she now needed to see, to touch, to hold, a desperate need, instinctual.

Out of the elevator, down the hall, into her room, then Natalie fell to her knees in front of the suitcase, pawing through it, pushing aside clothes and shoes and toiletries... and then her search became more frantic when that red velvet box was nowhere to be seen. She searched the suitcase once, twice, three times, her pulse racing, then the blood in her veins turned to ice as she realized the angel wasn't there.

The last gift from her parents, her most treasured possession. Gone.

CHAPTER 19

"It's here, honey. I went upstairs and had a look around your room, and sure enough, I found it right there in the nightstand, like you said."

Faith Holiday's voice was tinny over the phone, and Natalie sagged against her hotel room door in relief. After yet another round of frantic searching, she'd called The Mistletoe House—and then, when Faith hadn't answered, she'd called three more times, and left three increasingly panicked messages, until the innkeeper had finally returned her call. Somewhere along the way, she'd remembered that she left the angel by her bed at the inn, and in her haste to pack, she'd completely forgotten it was there.

"Today's Christmas Eve, so the post office is

closed, but I can ship it to you first thing on the 26th," Faith was saying as Natalie tried to catch her breath. "If you just give me your address, I'll write it down and—"

"No," Natalie cut in, shaking her head vigorously, though only she could see it. "No, I can't risk something happening to it in the mail. It could get lost, it could get broken, just... no." She glanced out her hotel window at the sky; snow clouds were looming overhead, and the day had turned gray and blustery. She estimated she had only a few hours left before the mountain roads around Chestnut Cove turned impassible, but if she left right now...

"I'm coming," she practically shouted into the phone as she embarked on a frenzied search for her car keys before finding them in her own pocket. "I'm coming right now." She yanked open her door and jogged down the hall. "Give me ninety minutes."

"Okay," Faith said, "but honey, I—"

But the rest of her sentence was cut off, because Natalie was already in the elevator, and her phone had lost its signal. She debated calling back, then decided against it. That would only slow her down, and right now, she didn't have a single second to waste.

THE SNOW WAS FALLING GENTLY by the time Natalie arrived in Chestnut Cove, though the meteorologists on the radio were gleefully predicting blizzard conditions by midnight. As she parked her car in front of The Mistletoe House, Natalie noticed that the cobblestone sidewalks in the town's main square were strangely empty, absent the usual hustle and bustle she'd witnessed in the lead-up to Christmas.

Most everyone was tucked up at home with their families, she suspected, enjoying the final hours of Christmas Eve, and a shroud of sadness clung to her as she slipped out from behind the wheel and headed toward the inn, alone. Somewhere in the distance, church bells began their slow, mournful toll, and it was with a heavy heart that she knocked once on the inn's front door before pushing it open and stepping inside.

A warm, cozy glow immediately descended on her, the flickering lights from the Christmas tree casting dancing shadows on the floor. Faith must have spent the afternoon baking, because the impossibly delicious scent of cookies filled the air, along with a hint of spiced cider. Breathing in deeply, Natalie made her way to the front desk, preparing to ring the bell to summon Faith before noticing a single sheet of paper beside it, her name printed across the top in the older woman's neat handwriting.

Natalie,

You left our conversation so quickly that I didn't have a chance to tell you I wouldn't be home today—I volunteered to set up the Christmas Eve community dinner at my church following this evening's service. I didn't want to leave your precious ornament unattended, so I've asked Gabe to keep it safe. He's waiting at his house for you whenever you arrive.

Merry Christmas, honey, and a blessed New Year.

Faith

Natalie read the note, then reread it twice more, her finger tracing over Gabe's name. She hadn't anticipated seeing him. In fact, she'd had no intentions of letting him know she was back in town. It was too painful, too unnecessary. Too brief. She had half a mind to ask Faith to mail the angel instead, but the thought of it getting lost or damaged was unbearable, and so she had no choice but to follow Faith's instructions. No choice but to come face to face with Gabe once again, and suddenly, as she stood in The Mistletoe House, surrounded by tinsel and lights and Santa Clauses and holiday cheer, that idea didn't seem like a tragedy.

It seemed like... an opportunity. Like fate. Like maybe, just maybe, it was meant to happen this way all along.

"Thanks, Mom," she whispered to the Christmas tree, knowing instinctually that they could hear her. That they were out there somewhere, waiting, watching. "Thanks, Daddy."

Then Natalie tucked the note into the pocket of her coat for safekeeping before turning on her heel and hurrying back to her car. The soft glow of twilight was descending over Chestnut Cove as she drove through the quiet streets, the coral rays of sunset giving way to a dusky mauve that provided a showstopping backdrop to the snowcapped mountains surrounding the town she'd come to love. Her heart was beating dully at the base of her throat as she pulled up to Gabe's cabin and parked behind his pickup truck, gripping the steering wheel and taking deep, steadying breaths, her mind racing, her head and her heart at odds with each other...

No, Natalie realized, quite abruptly. No. For the first time since she'd met him, there was no internal battle waging, no push-and-pull, no war between what she wanted—quietly, desperately—and what she feared. There was just... peace. For once, there was just peace.

Knot of anticipation in her stomach, tiniest flicker of hope in her soul, she climbed the steps to Gabe's front porch—

And only when she raised a hand to knock on the door did she realize that something was wrong. Different, and wrong, and very, very *wrong*.

There were no lights strung around the pine trees outside, no candles glowing softly in the windows. No wreath adorning the door, no snowman family waving from the front yard. No Santa Claus on the roof, no twinkling reindeer in the front yard. Instead, the exterior of Gabe's house was entirely bare.

Frowning, feeling slightly panicked but not entirely sure why, Natalie banged on the door repeatedly until she heard footsteps approaching on the other side. The door swung open, and Gabe was standing there, and in a single moment of vulnerability, she saw the hope in his eyes—and the uncertainty, too, the fear that she was going to leave again. This time, permanently, like she had promised.

"Hi," he whispered, his gaze never leaving her face.

A beat while she stared at him, unable to tear her eyes away from his. "Hi."

He stepped back from the door. "Did you want to come in?" he asked, his voice hesitant. "Faith dropped off your angel a little while ago. She told me what happened—I'm sorry you had to drive all the way back here."

Ignoring this, Natalie gestured behind her to the front yard. "Where are all your Christmas decorations?" Then, glancing inside the cabin for the first time, she saw that every last surface was bare. Everything was gone. Everything. There was no sign of Christmas anywhere, other than the tree in the corner—bare except for a wilting star, its lights in a tangle at its base.

Breath hitching at the base of her throat, she stared at him. "Why?"

He took a step toward her, his eyes locked on hers, misery etched on every inch of his face. "Natalie... please," he said, his voice low, rough. "Please, just listen to me. I love Christmas—I've always loved Christmas, but... but I fell in love with you." He took her hand, and electricity zinged down her spine. "And that's more important to me than any holiday. *You're* more important to me than any holiday. If you take me back, Natalie, I swear, I'll never utter the word 'Christmas' in your presence again. I'll never decorate the house, or trim the tree, or do any of those things, because at the end of the day, I know with everything I have that you are my soulmate. You are my person. And that will always, *always*, be enough."

He took another step toward her, his face desperate. "So please, Natalie. Please, come inside. Please, just… stay." He reached for her, but Natalie took a step back, away from his touch, and his hand grasped only air instead. The hope was gone from his eyes in an instant; his expression shuttered.

"No," Natalie said softly, shaking her head. "No, Gabe, that's not what I want. That's not who you are." It was her turn to move closer to him, and the hope on his face reignited, his soul was laid bare at her feet, and the air around them took on a shimmering quality, charged, electric in its intensity.

When she spoke next, her voice was soft but firm. "On the drive here—and for the past few days, really —I've had a chance to think about things. I've had a chance to remember, and I know, I *know*, that this life, the one I've been living… it's not the one my parents would have wanted for me. And more importantly, it's not the one I want for myself." Her eyes were blazing into his, and he didn't look away, didn't even blink, as if he didn't dare to break the connection.

"I loved Christmas," she said, a single tear slipping down her cheek. "I loved it then, and I think... I think I could love it again, if I give myself a chance. If I take things slowly... very, *very* slowly," she said with a laugh, closing her eyes against Gabe's touch as he reached out to brush away her tears.

She caught his hand before he could withdraw it, and held on tight. "Will you help me do that, Gabe?" she whispered. "Will you help me try?" She swallowed hard. "And if I fail, will you just... be with me? And tell me it's okay?"

He nodded solemnly. "I will. I promise you, Natalie, I swear it—I will."

She didn't respond. Instead, she stepped around him, reaching for the velvet box on the table beside the front door, the one that contained the most precious thing she possessed. She lifted the lid, a smile curving her lips as she gazed down at that little angel, so plain yet so beautiful, wondrous, a true miracle, a message from the beyond. Then she removed it from the box and walked over to the bare tree, standing on tiptoe as she gently, reverently, raised it to the very top, hanging it in a place of honor just below the star.

"Your new home," she whispered, stepping back to admire the effect, the tears falling freely down her face—tears for everything she had lost, all the pain, the sadness, the grief she had endured, but tears of hope, too, and the promise of a better future, brighter, filled with happiness and light. And above all, filled with love. The kind of love that only came around once in a lifetime, the kind of love meant to last. The kind of love that could move mountains, and bring back the magic of Christmas to a little girl who lost it so long ago.

She didn't know when Gabe came to stand behind her, but suddenly his arms were around her, safe, secure, and she leaned into him briefly before turning to face him, stroking his hair, his face, reveling in this man, this love, this perfect moment.

"Merry Christmas, Gabe," she whispered.

He brushed away the last of her tears, then cupped her face in his hands, his eyes bright. "Merry Christmas, Natalie."

The first kiss was a tentative brush of lips, warm and soft, perfect, but the one that followed?

Well, that was a kiss that made the angels sing.

"*K*nock, knock!" Faith shouldered open the door, her arms weighed down with an enormous platter of what looked to be at least two hundred Christmas cookies in every imaginable variety: thumbprints and peanut blossoms, lady locks and gingerbread men. No, gingerbread *babies*, Natalie noted with glee, waddling over to Faith and lifting the platter from her hands.

"Do you like them?" Faith asked, grinning down at the icing bonnets adorning the gingerbread babies. "Holly thought I was nuts when I made the request, but she came around... especially when I reminded her that she would be the baby's favorite aunt."

"And what will *you* be?" Gabe asked from his perch atop a ladder. He had spent the past two hours hanging baby Santa Claus, reindeer, and elf decorations from the doorways, in addition to the food he had prepared and the fresh pine tree he had cut down just that morning. Despite Natalie's protests that he was working too hard, he assured her that he didn't mind—that he'd waited years for this time in his life, and now that it was here, he was going to soak up every second of it.

"I'll be the baby's fairy godmother, of course," Faith said, wandering around the cabin, nodding in approval as she took in the decorations. "Spoiling her rotten at every available opportunity." A Christmas-themed baby shower had been Faith's idea, and Natalie had happily agreed. None of the guests who were attending the event seemed to care that the holidays were still several months away; they had been thrilled to learn that Natalie and Gabe were expecting their firstborn on Christmas day.

"I have a better idea," Gabe said, stepping down from the ladder and crossing the room to kiss Faith on the cheek. He and Natalie shared a smile over her shoulder, Natalie's hand automatically resting on her growing belly, protecting the precious life inside. "We've talked about it," he said, gesturing between himself and his wife, "and we thought, if you're up for it... we thought you might like to be her honorary grandmother."

Faith stared at him for a long moment, speechless, and then her eyes welled up with tears. "Look at me, crying like a baby before the actual baby's even born," she said with a laugh, dabbing at her cheeks with the hem of her shirt. Then she turned to embrace both Gabe and Natalie in turn. "It would be the honor of my life," she whispered, her voice catching. She leaned back, brushing her fingers against Natalie's cheek. "I'll do your mother proud."

Natalie caught her hand and squeezed it. "I don't doubt that you will." Then she gave the older woman a sly grin. "And I even have your first grandmotherly task, because yes, this role does come with homework."

"More homework than planning you a baby shower?" Faith grumbled good-naturedly, unable to keep the grin from her face. Then, more seriously, "How can I help you, honey?"

"You can help me," Natalie said, plopping onto the sofa with an *oof* and a wince, "by going through these baby name books with me. I've read through each of them at least half a dozen times, and for the life of me, I can't make a decision." She gestured toward a stack of books on the coffee table, each featuring an adorable baby on the cover, and groaned. "I'm about to spin right off the planet."

"I can most definitely help with that." Faith took a seat beside Natalie on the sofa, gingerly, so as not to jostle her around too much… which was impossible, Natalie thought, because even now, at six months pregnant, she had reached roughly the size and weight of a baby whale. The older woman removed the topmost book from the stack and began to flip through it, her eyes scanning the endless list of names and their meanings.

"Oh, Gabe," she called out a few seconds later, "I've been meaning to tell you, we're having the first planning meeting for this year's Santa's Wonderland next Tuesday. Can Walter and I count on you to help with the decorations again?"

"You bet," he replied in a muffled voice, his nose half-buried in the tree he was now stringing with garland fashioned out of rolled-up diapers—another of Faith's creations. "Just name the date and time, and I'll be there."

"And you'd better hope your friend Jeannie doesn't come down with the flu again," Natalie chimed in, glancing up from the baby name book she'd been perusing. "Because there's no way I'm fitting into that elf costume *this* year, or standing on my feet for so long. I already had to cut back on my hours at Miller Farm, and the baby isn't due for months yet."

Several beats of silence followed, and then Gabe and Faith shared a look before the two of them burst out laughing. Natalie glanced back and forth between her husband and her friend, nonplussed. "I don't get it. What's so funny?"

"Oh, honey," Faith said, laying a hand on Natalie's shoulder, her eyes still bright with laughter. "Didn't I ever tell you? There's no Jeannie in this town. I made her up."

"Why?" Natalie asked, gaping at the older woman. "What made you do that?"

Faith's expression turned solemn. "Because when you landed on my doorstep, I took one look at you and knew you needed some joy in your life. And that one over there?" She nodded toward Gabe, who was grinning sheepishly. Faith shrugged. "He took one look at you... and he knew you needed to stay."

Natalie was quiet for a moment, her mind wandering over the events of the past nine months—the fears, the insecurities, the grief. The loneliness, the heartache. And then that first spark of hope that led to a future more beautiful than she could have ever imagined.

And now…

Faith was looking at her hesitantly, chewing on her bottom lip with worry. "Oh, honey, you're not mad, are you?"

"Mad?" Natalie asked in disbelief. "How could I be mad?" She wrapped her arms around the older woman. "You helped make every one of my dreams come true, Faith. And now, you've helped me come up with the perfect name for our daughter." She met Gabe's eyes from across the room, and he nodded, his gaze soft, adoring. He was a wonderful husband, and would be an even more wonderful father, Natalie knew.

With tears in her eyes, she rested her hand on her belly once more. "You finally have a name, sweet girl," she murmured. "Everyone, I'd like you to meet Jeannie." She grinned at Gabe, her heart glowing with happiness, the familiar butterflies in her stomach taking flight. "Jeannie Noelle Archer, our very own Christmas miracle."

DEAR READER,

I hope you enjoyed *The Mistletoe House*! For another cozy, heartfelt Christmas romance set in the beautiful mountain town of Chestnut Cove, I hope you'll join me for the second book in the series, **The Mistletoe Wish**.

Want to be a VIP Reader? Join my Reader Club for all the latest news on upcoming releases, special savings, fun announcements, sneak peeks, and more —delivered right to your inbox! Visit www.miakent. com/readerclub to sign up.

Thank you so much for your support!

Love,

Mia

ABOUT THE AUTHOR

Mia Kent is the author of clean, contemporary women's fiction and small-town romance. She writes heartfelt stories about love, friendship, happily ever after, and the importance of staying true to yourself.

She's been married for over a decade to her high school sweetheart, and when she isn't working on her next book, she's chasing around a toddler, crawling after an infant, and hiding from an eighty-pound tornado of dog love. Frankly, it's a wonder she writes at all.

To learn more about Mia's books, to sign up for her email list, or to send her a message, visit her website at www.miakent.com.